LIFE WITH THE AFTERLIFE

STORIES OF LIFE AFTER DEATH, SECOND CHANCES, AND ENDURING LOVE

ROBIN BRANDE

RYER PUBLISHING

LIFE WITH THE AFTERLIFE:

Stories of Life After Death, Second Chances, and Enduring Love

By Robin Brande

Published by Ryer Publishing
www.ryerpublishing.com
© 2025 Robin Brande
www.robinbrande.com
All rights reserved.
Cover art by Chainver-gallery/Canva
Ebook ISBN: 978-1-952383-63-2
Print ISBN: 978-1-952383-64-9

"The Calling" first appeared in the book *The Love of a Good Dog* by Robin Brande.

"Believer" first appeared in the book *Believer* by Robin Brande, part of the Dove Season Universe.

"The Bridge" first appeared in *Pulphouse Magazine* #14.

"Second Life" first appeared in the book *Maker* by Robin Brande, part of the Dove Season Universe.

"From the Bones of a Good Dog" first appeared in the book *The Love of a Good Dog* by Robin Brande.

ALSO BY ROBIN BRANDE

<u>Winnie Parsons Mysteries</u>

A Mind for Mysteries (Collection)

The Genius Track

A Man of Appetites

A Drop of Sweat

The Long Gray Hook

The Slip of a Rib

The Cabin Ghost

The Secret Juror

<u>Dove Season Universe</u>

Dove Season

Finder

Seeker

Believer

Maker

Explorer

<u>Young Adult</u>

Evolution, Me & Other Freaks of Nature

Fat Cat

Doggirl

Replay

Into the Parallel

Caught in the Parallel

Seize the Parallel

Beyond the Parallel

Book of Earth

Book of Water

<u>Romance</u>

Love Proof

Freefall

Heart of Ice

Fire and Ice

<u>Self-Help</u>

What If You're Doing It Right?

What If You're Doing It Right? For Teens

<u>Collections</u>

The Love of a Good Dog

Mountain Tough

The Miraculous Unknown

Life with the Afterlife

LIFE WITH THE AFTERLIFE

CONTENTS

THE CALLING

INTRODUCTION

Veterinarian Drianne has always had a special connection with her patients. Some might call it a gift.

Dogs and cats seem to know her, even if she has never met them before. And she swears she can sometimes guess what they are thinking and feeling.

There is more to Drianne's gift with animals than she realizes.

A story of the enduring love between people and their animals.

1

———————

Surgery days were always stressful.

Even just spays and neuters, even though people thought of them as routine, were still opening up a body. Owners dropped off their dogs and cats in the morning thinking they would just go grab a coffee while the deed was done, and the animal would be good to go within about an hour. Like it was factory work.

But for Drianne it was anything but routine.

Almost fifty years old now, she had been a vet for twenty years. And she still sweated every time she sliced open a living, breathing body. It was sacred work, having an animal in her hands.

It was a calling she was too afraid to heed for the first half of her twenties. For the most part because her biology teacher in high school had scoffed at the idea.

"You could never pass the classes," he told her. "Vet school is rigorous. You're failing my class and this is easy."

Those words defined her for so long. She majored in English instead. Compromised.

Gave up.

Turned her ship toward becoming a teacher. A noble calling all its own, even though it wasn't hers.

It wasn't until she was driving her grandfather to one of his final cancer treatments that someone managed to break the spell.

"You should do what you want," he rasped through his tumor-ridden throat. "Don't listen to anyone. You can do whatever you put your mind to. You're a smart girl, Drianne."

If he had said it to her a year before, at a family barbeque or Christmas brunch, she wouldn't have given it so much weight.

But he died just a few weeks later. It became a kind of directive. The last words of a dying man.

At least that's what Drianne told herself. Because if she admitted she was doing it because it was what she had wanted to do since she was six, then that high school biology teacher's words would have won. He had already kept her away from her dream all the way through college.

But Granddad, he was a serious and driven man.

If he told Drianne to do it, she'd damn well better do it.

So she started over. And the classes were hard, no question.

But she also found a kind of grace that overlaid them.

With each test she took, Drianne felt a hand guiding her own as it filled in test answer bubbles or wrote out longer explanations on the page.

The lectures were complicated. But her ears adjusted almost right away. Like there was a translator inside her head, taking scientific concepts and turning them into real dogs and cats and horses.

Drianne could picture the diseases. The injuries.

She could see her own healing hands.

She could imagine the faces of little girls and boys, so worried when they brought in their sick animals, so elated when Drianne returned them well.

She could smell the fur. See the soft and inquisitive eyes. Each class was a new experience in meeting all the animals of Drianne's imagination. Every hour brought a new set of creatures she could imagine petting and examining and helping.

The day she graduated from vet school she felt a strong grip on her right shoulder. She was standing on the stage with the other graduates, and whipped around to see who had touched her.

No one was there. Not in the flesh.

She lowered her chin so no one would see her lips move.

"Thank you, Granddad."

She had offers from practices in bigger cities, but she wanted to stay where she was.

Rural Colorado, a small college town called Greeley, near the countryside where her ancestors had been homesteaders who built their own farms and farmhouses by hand.

Eventually the generations evolved toward more suburban lives. Drianne's mother was an accountant. Her father was an engineer.

Anyone else, other than her high school biology teacher, would have looked at those genetics and assumed Drianne would be great at a science career.

But expectations could be a burden. Whether they were expectations of failure or success.

For the past twenty years Drianne had been learning to ignore expectations and instead follow her heart.

Right now her heart was breaking.

She had an old dog on the surgical table. A fourteen-year-old black Lab named Bear. A good old boy, slow and stiff, but still with life in him. Drianne had known him for many years.

The owners, a retired couple named the Baxters who had raised Bear from a puppy, said the dog still loved his slow walks, sniffing every leaf of every bush, still enjoyed his food, even though it seemed it was getting harder for him to eat.

They thought it might be because of a broken canine tooth that looked infected. They asked Drianne to take a look.

But it was worse than that. Once Drianne pried Bear's mouth open, she could see the mass inside. The size of a golf ball, growing down from the roof of his mouth.

But she had done mouth surgeries before. Hundreds.

"I can get that out," she told the Baxters with confidence. "We can at least make him more comfortable for a while. His blood work looks good. He could have another year."

But once she got him on the table this morning, she knew at most he'd have another week.

The mass had grown so much over the weekend, it was clear the malignancy was going to cut off his airway within days. That was a horrible way to go.

A sweet old dog like this deserved better. She was relieved that the Baxters saw it the same way.

"I can wake him up," Drianne said when she called them. "Give you another few days."

"If he's sleeping now," Rella Baxter said, her voice choked with tears, "let's let him sleep. We'll be there soon to say goodbye."

Drianne had a room set aside for the terminal

patients. More like a bedroom than a treatment room. Soft lighting. Candles. A comfortable couch.

One of her vet techs rolled the mobile unit that continued to pipe in anesthesia, while the other helped Drianne carry the old dog from the surgical table into the special room and onto the couch.

Drianne put a pillow under Bear's head. His tongue lolled out of his mouth, past the breathing tube, but he looked so sweet. Peaceful. His paw even twitched sometimes while he dreamed.

The Baxters arrived, crying. Drianne told them exactly what she saw when she looked inside. Dave Baxter cried softly into his fist. Rella petted her dog and kissed his face.

"He's been sleeping about twenty-two hours a day lately," Dave said.

Drianne smiled at him gently. "And now he'll get to sleep twenty-four."

When it was time, when they were ready, Drianne administered the three successive shots. Dave Baxter had left by then, he couldn't be there, but Rella stayed on until the end.

As Drianne pushed the first syringe, she spoke to the old dog, knowing he could hear.

"You were a good boy, Bear. One of the best. Now go find another body."

Rella wept quietly, touched by those final words.

But Drianne didn't say the words lightly.
She knew by now what they could do.

2

It took a few years into her practice before she began to notice a pattern.

Puppies who leaped from their owners' arms and came bounding toward Drianne as if they knew her.

Kittens who purred so loudly when she held them, the owners often laughed at how unusually vocal they were.

Dogs she met on the street who rushed to her, tails wagging like mad, desperate for Drianne to pet them.

She had always had a way with animals. But this felt like something more.

She was at a veterinarian conference in Denver one year when she mentioned it to one of the other attendees.

The vet, a woman named Linda who had long gray hair and light blue eyes, gave Drianne a peculiar look.

"Let me ask you something," Linda said. "When you put an animal down, do you say anything?"

Drianne shrugged. "Sometimes. If I know them."

"What do you say?" Linda asked.

"I tell them they've been good. And that I hope they come back some day."

Linda smiled. "Do you now."

Drianne felt self-conscious. "It's just ... something to say. Why, what do you do?"

"Oh, I have a whole conversation," Linda said. "But only if I like the animal. If it's a biter or screamer or scratcher, forget it."

Drianne chuckled nervously. She wasn't sure anymore that they were talking about the same thing.

"What do you tell them?" Drianne asked. "The ones that you like?"

"That they should go find another body," Linda answered. "And nine times out of ten, they do."

Drianne stared at her a moment, not quite sure if this was a joke.

"Not all of us can do it," Linda told her. "Not everybody has the connection. But if you do..." She tipped back her plastic cup and drank the last of her red wine. "You should meet a few people while you're here. You might be interested."

3

Looking around at the mostly gray-haired group, Drianne felt distinctly young and underqualified. She was only thirty-five then, in her fifth year of practice. These vets looked like they had been practicing for decades.

There were about a dozen of them standing at one side of the conference room while hundreds of other attendees milled around and mingled.

Linda introduced her. Drianne tried hard to remember everyone's names.

They were men and women from all over the country. Gary, Indiana. Paloma, California. Chicago. Santa Fe. Provo, Utah. Cincinnati. Some with big city practices, some with small rural practices like hers.

After Linda finished the introductions, she lowered her voice and leaned closer to Drianne.

"We've all got the talent," she said.

Drianne assumed it was a slight brag. Telling her that these vets were all experts at what they did.

"I'm sure," Drianne answered politely.

An older woman who looked like she might be eighty reached out her soft hand and gripped Drianne's arm. "She means the special connection. Moving the animals on."

"Encouraging them to come back," Linda said.

Drianne was only on the brink of understanding. But before she could ask anything else, the vet from Gary, Indiana broke in. Drianne had already forgotten his name. She thought of him as simply Gary.

"Did you ever read about the Siberian fox study?" he asked.

"You mean ... about domestication?" she said.

"Right," Gary said. "Back in the 1950s a couple of Russian scientists captured hundreds of wild foxes, then chose only the most docile, friendly ones to breed. The ones the scientists could touch without the foxes biting. Within a few years, they had a whole generation of foxes who would lick their faces and follow them around like puppies."

"That's what we're doing," Linda told her. "Those of us who the animals can hear. Every time we have to euthanize one of our favorite dogs or cats, we tell them to find new bodies and come back."

"It's our own way of evolving the species," Gary said. "Making sure we have more of the kinds of animals we all love. Fewer of the crazy ones and the biters."

Drianne almost laughed. It was too unbelievable. But as she gazed around at the group of seasoned veterinarians, she saw that many of them were nodding, their expressions serious. The rest were listening comfortably as if all of this bizarre information were all completely known and normal.

"You said you've seen young animals who seem to know you," Linda said.

"Y-yes," Drianne said.

"Of course they remember you," the soft-handed woman in her eighties said. "You were kind to them. Animals want only the most loving vets, too."

"So ... you can all do this," Drianne said, looking around at the group.

"And you," Linda told her, "I'll bet. But there aren't very many of us. I'm always on the lookout at these conferences for more." She gestured toward her silver-haired colleagues. "We're a dying breed. We need new blood. I hope you'll go home and try it, and then tell us what happens."

4

In the days following the conference, Drianne felt as though she had stepped into an alternate universe. One where vets had powers she'd never imagined.

But of course she wanted to try.

It was the most exciting thing she'd ever heard.

Euthanizing animals had always been the worst aspect of her practice. People expected her to be stoic. Detached. Unemotional.

But she often had to leave the room right away after administering the drugs, to go have a private cry behind the closed door of her office.

Helping an animal die was a sacred duty to her. She wanted it to be as easy and as loving as possible. But it was still taking a life. She would never think of that as routine.

But now. Now she had a new appreciation for her role.

And new hope that she might do something more than just ease an animal out of its suffering.

She had an opportunity to try it just a week later.

Agnes was a beautiful old gray and white Maine Coon cat belonging to one of Drianne's favorite owners. Tracy Morrow had strung out the end as long as she could.

But finally Agnes wasn't eating or drinking anymore. And when she walked, it was clear the cat was in terrible pain.

"I could wait for her to go naturally," Tracy said. "But what if the pain keeps getting worse? I can't do that to her. It's not fair."

She sat with Agnes sleeping on her lap. The cat's normally well-groomed thick fur looked ragged and matted.

Agnes continued sleeping while Drianne began to examine her.

When she lightly touched the cat's belly, Agnes's eyes flew open and she hissed.

Tracy began to cry. "Please. I can't let her hurt another night."

Drianne prepared the three shots. She knelt in front of the chair where Tracy held sweet Agnes on her lap.

"You've been a good girl," Drianne said as the needle penetrated the vein in Agnes's front leg. "Thank you for letting us know you. Now go find another body."

Tracy wept at those words. She held Agnes to her chest while Drianne administered the remaining shots.

Drianne laid her stethoscope gently against Agnes's heart.

"Look how peaceful," she whispered. "She's gone."

Drianne left the two of them alone in the room.

This time Drianne didn't feel the urge to cry.

Instead she hurried to write in the private journal she had bought, recording Agnes's name and the date and some details about her personality and her life.

Then Drianne waited. While months went by.

In the fall, she saw Tracy Morrow listed on her schedule for the day.

A new kitten. Another Maine Coon.

Drianne knew it from the moment she entered the examination room.

The kitten started meowing at her so energetically, nonstop, it made Tracy laugh out loud.

"Well!" she said. "Guess Miss Abigail has something to say!"

But it was the kitten's gorgeous green eyes, boring so intensely into Drianne's, that made her know the two of them had known each other before.

"Hello, beautiful," Drianne said, taking the kitten from Tracy's arms.

She turned away so the owner wouldn't hear. She whispered into the kitten's ear, "Welcome back."

5

Now, fifteen years later, Drianne still treated many of her former patients.

Her favorite Labradors with their sweet, goofy smiles.

A mixed-breed shelter dog who was once a Golden Retriever who saved the family's young daughter from drowning in the lake.

The Bernese Mountain Dog who was once a Dachshund who must have dreamed of being a big dog for a change.

Cats who had lived their full lives and brought joy and love every day to their owners. Now back as playful kittens with enough fresh energy to carry them through another full and joyful life.

And even though some owners vowed they could never get another dog or cat, that it was too painful to say goodbye, Drianne heard time and again about the coincidences.

"I was just walking by…"

"My neighbor's cat had kittens. As soon as I saw them, I couldn't resist…"

"This fella just jumped right into my lap! How was I gonna say no?"

Drianne sometimes had to excuse herself, pretend she needed a fresh thermometer or some other equipment, just so she could stand in the hallway outside the exam room and allow a few tears to fall.

The animals missed their owners, too. That much was clear. It wasn't just Drianne directing the show. Maybe some of them would have made their way back on their own, even if she never told them to find new bodies.

Those animals felt their own calling. To bring joy to these particular people.

Like the Siberian fox experiment in reverse. Sweet animals helping the human race evolve over time, making them happier and kinder, one person at a time.

Drianne's private journal was now several volumes long. She sent regular reports to the rest of the vets in her special group.

Many of the old ones were gone now. But Drianne and Linda had been finding and recruiting others at the annual conferences.

More vets with the special connection. The special breed who could communicate with their dying patients.

It was sacred work, Drianne told them, having an animal's life in your hands.

All the more sacred when you could welcome them back.

As sacred as being a high school biology teacher who could encourage a young woman to follow this path.

Or could almost rob her of her true calling with just a few cruel and thoughtless words.

Words carried power. Drianne never doubted it anymore.

Words from a grandfather. *"You can do whatever you put your mind to. You're a smart girl, Drianne."*

Or from the veterinarian whose job it was to offer a peaceful goodbye. Even though ending the life of a precious animal still always left a pain in her heart.

They might come back—she hoped they did—but *this* animal, *this* version ... she would never see exactly this one ever again.

It was why tears still gathered in her eyes when she had to help one of her favorites go.

But now she also knew to wait. The joy would come again.

From a Persian who was now a scrawny feral cat who had to travel miles to find his human again.

From a gangly mutt someone got from the pound,

who used to be a majestic old Collie that Drianne still missed.

All of them answering the Calling in their hearts.

That calling was love. Love between animals and their humans.

It never got old. She never got tired of it. This work was what she was meant to do.

Drianne turned out the lights at her clinic.

Knowing this place would call her back in the morning.

BRINDLE

INTRODUCTION

On a remote farm a mysterious little girl named Brindle survives against all odds.

Her mother is dead. Her grandparents refuse to raise her. Still the girl lives on.

What is her secret? Her grandparents are desperate to know. Because they have a secret of their own.

But as they discover, some kinds of love create powerful magic.

A fantasy tale about life, death, and love.

BRINDLE

Brindle was as thin as broth. She lived by the grace of a nanny goat's milk and the timothy grass in the pasture. She was as soft and pale as a chick. She had been fading away to nothing from the day she was born.

"Oh, Lord," Brindle's grandfather moaned. He had heard the cries in the darkness. A fallen lamb, he thought, so he rushed, but he found his unmarried daughter instead. Fornicator. Finally her sin was upon her. She lay dead in the pasture, her newborn infant suckling the last of the milk through the threadbare cloth of her mother's nightdress.

"Oh Lord," and he cut the cord.

Grandfather carried Brindle to the dirty floor of the barn, expecting to rake her out with the mud and straw in the morning.

Brindle survived her first night, and then, unmercifully, others.

"It's a Test," Grandfather said.

"What should we do?" Grandmother asked.

Grandfather read in his Holy Book: If a beggar asks for your shirt, offer your cloak as well.

So they took a rotting cloak from a corner of the damp barn and laid it near the baby—not on her, but close enough that the Lord might intervene if He felt that was the right thing to do.

They laid a platter of crumbs near the infant, but made no effort to feed her themselves.

"Surely the Lord should be expected to do His part," the grandparents agreed.

The child persisted in living.

They glanced into the barn only now and then, just to see whether it was time to dig a second grave, and reminded themselves that Patience was the Lord's own gift.

"Job had the sores upon his body," Grandfather consoled his wife. "Surely we can bear up a little longer."

And longer. Years took their time in passing. Occasionally, against their will, the grandparents would spy the child romping in the meadow flowers with the lambs and the kids. Brindle seemed as light as the stars. She behaved as though she had no shame—as though she were not shame itself. Catching sight of her brought scowls and sharp words between the grandfolk. Her innocent smile ruined what would otherwise have been a pleasant day.

"That child sets me off," Grandmother confessed. "It's not right."

"It is a hard Test," Grandfather agreed, "but the Lord is merciful. The harder the Test, the greater the Reward."

By the time she was seven, Brindle was even lovelier than her mother had been. Brindle's hair turned a gentle curly white, like milk at the top of the pail. Her legs were as long as a fawn's. She laughed often and easily. She might even have learned a word or two somewhere—no one could really be sure. The grandparents did all they could not to look at her anymore, but the more they disciplined themselves to ignore her, the harder that became.

Because something strange was happening.

When they did look—furtively, guiltily, afraid that someone might catch them—when they did look, they could not see Brindle at all. She was there at the corner of their eyes, but if they turned—no matter how quickly— she was gone. They did not want to stare too long, even if it were to solve this mystery, but the impulse to see her— to really see her—was maddening.

At first neither mentioned this fact to the other. Each stole a moment from every day, and each had the same sensation: The child, soft and light, was there smiling at something in her hand, but the moment they tried to focus their gaze, the child vanished.

"Mother," Grandfather finally ventured one night.

"Yes?" she answered nervously. She had considered addressing the matter herself that very night, and now hoped she would not have to.

Grandfather cleared his throat.

"Yes?" Grandmother prompted him.

"I think," he said, averting his eyes and concentrating on the lamb pie on his plate, "we need to burn the barn."

"Yes, exactly," she answered. "A fresh start."

"Exactly," he said.

When supper was over, and Grandmother was in her warm nightdress, Grandfather coughed slightly and mumbled something and gathered his heavy coat and gloves.

"Hat," Grandmother barely whispered. "It's so cold tonight."

Properly bundled, Grandfather made his way across the yard. He had never been to the barn after dark since that first night, when he had laid the pale infant on top of the straw and left the door slightly ajar for any wild thing to come and carry her away.

He shined the light from his lantern into the corners of the barn. The animals stirred some, but Grandfather cooed for them to settle.

"Little one?" he called tentatively. "Little one, are you here?"

He wished he had more light. He swung the lantern in a circle, looking behind in case the child was sneaking up on him. Horses shifted in their stalls. A cow moaned for him to douse the light.

There. Was that her? He thought for a moment he saw her ... but no, nothing. He scolded himself. Why did he expect to see her now, this time? Of course she was there —where else would she be? What was he waiting for?

He tipped his lantern onto the straw and backed away toward the barn door. Fire fed on the tinder. Soon there was a handy blaze.

Brindle emerged shyly from the shadows, and Grandfather could not help but see her. The girl knelt on the straw and stretched out her hands over the flames. "Thank you, Grandfather," she said softly. "I was so cold tonight."

"Lord!" Grandfather twisted away and scuttled toward the house, the child's eyes still burning in his own. He bolted the door behind him and edged toward the window. Upstairs in her bedroom, Grandmother watched as well. They watched throughout the night, but nothing came of the flames. In the morning, bleary-eyed, Grandfather stumbled toward the barn.

Brindle sat on the straw, still warming her hands over

the cheerful fire. She smiled brilliantly when he looked in on her.

Brindle smiled and opened her hand. "Grandfather, come and see. Look who it is."

He did not look. If he had, he would have seen a tiny bead on Brindle's palm. And inside the bead, a light that glowed gentle white. If he had looked at it directly, the light would have faded away, and all he would see was a dull gray pebble. But if he had looked at it from the corners of his eyes he would have seen inside the Heavens and watched Brindle's mother dance along golden streets.

"She comes when I call," Brindle said softly. "She holds me in her arms. She came to me last night—"

"No!" Grandfather fled back into the house.

Grandmother awaited word.

"No," her husband said. "No, damn you! She's still there."

Grandmother's eyes burned with tears. "How much longer?" she wailed, addressing the Heavens and not her husband. "I am a righteous woman! What did I do wrong? Where is the Lord when I call?"

Ah, the night before had been so cold. Brindle had sat in the darkness and called to her mother, "Please come. Mother, please hold me."

"Sweet babe," her young mother answered. She wrapped Brindle tightly in her arms. "You are so very cold tonight. I will find you a warm fire. See, here comes my father now with the lantern. The Lord will always provide."

BELIEVER

INTRODUCTION

Analyst Alice Kern wants the truth about her parents' murder—but only the truth.

Now her colleague from the Agency has a new source of information.

But is this mysterious woman reliable?

Or is she just another pretender claiming she can see into the past?

A tale of intrigue, grief, and the hope that those we love are never truly gone.

Meeting at forty-one thousand feet made the most sense.

Alice Kern sat in one of the soft tan leather seats inside Major Zimholt's private jet and waited for her former colleague from the Agency, Gina Firenzi, to hurry aboard.

Even after six consecutive months of doing it this way, Alice was still always tense during the pickups and drop-offs. Four different assassins had already tried to kill her in the space of one week last December—why, Alice still didn't know—and there was always a moment before Gina's tall Amazon-like frame filled the jet doorway when Alice wondered if someone else would appear instead and try to gun her down.

It was why she, the pilot Arnie Camper, and the cabin steward Bruce always came armed on the flight.

Gina would be carrying too, ready in case anyone might be waiting for her when she deplaned a few hours later. She had already taken a knife in her back last December from one of the assassins trying to get past her on his way to Alice. And someone else had tried to kill Gina just a few weeks after that while she pursued one of Alice's leads.

As careful as the two of them tried to be, there was always obviously a risk. But the meetings were too important to miss. Alice and Gina had made real progress in their investigations over the past few months. And they could no longer communicate through the Agency network. Alice had learned her lesson. That was how at least one of the assassins had found where she was hiding at what was supposed to be a secure military base.

Using his jet had been Major Zimholt's idea. A place for Alice and Gina to meet face-to-face, without having to go somewhere public where they might be followed.

Alice had been surprised when Gina first reached out to her back in February, in part because Alice assumed the Agency was done with her. She hadn't heard from anyone at her old job since she went underground with Major Zimholt's group. No one was paying her salary anymore. No one was checking in. She wondered if the Factory,

Major Zimholt's hidden facility in the Wasatch Mountain Range above Salt Lake City, Utah, was really so secure that no one even from Agency could find out where she was.

Alice adjusted to her new, isolated workplace. She spent her days doing exactly what she had been doing before as an analyst: delving into research, following leads, trying to understand the larger picture of who was behind the murder of her parents by creating a mosaic of smaller, sometimes random-appearing pieces. Without access to the Agency's extensive network, she could no longer follow live investigations, but the Factory had its own internal database that was filling in pieces Alice didn't even know she was missing.

Including the secret her parents had been keeping from her all of Alice's life. But there was even more to know than that. Always more. Alice kept following the bread crumbs.

Then one day Arnie Camper gave a quick knock on the door of the second-floor computer room and stuck his head in.

"Message for you," he said in greeting. Camper always had places to go, things to do. He didn't waste his words. He was a test pilot both for the military, at a secret base called the Aviary, and at the Factory, flying Major Zimholt's experimental crafts. He also occasionally piloted Major Zimholt's private jet.

"Gina Firenzi wants a meet," Camper said. "This week. Up for it?"

"Y-yeah," Alice said in surprise. But it was a good surprise. She didn't know Gina well, but she liked her. She liked the senior investigator's confidence. And even though Alice had been the one to kill the assassin who attacked Gina and then her, Gina seemed competent and safe. Alice had the feeling Gina Firenzi was someone reliable to have around in a crisis.

"Any day," Alice told Camper. "Thursday?"

"Thursday," he confirmed. "Nine." Then he shut the door on the computer room and was gone.

Thursday morning Alice was ready early, not really knowing what to expect. She had coffee and a banana and was showered and dressed by eight. She could see from the camera feed showing the weather outside the Factory that the sunlight was still barely creeping over the top of the mountains. The temperature was below zero. She waited in her room until she couldn't stand just sitting around any longer. Freezing or not, she would rather head outside and wait for the sunshine. She bundled up and went.

She had left her old apartment back in San Diego in a hurry, after shooting the first of the series of assassins, the one who broke in during the middle of the night. Although later someone from the Agency had packed a garbage bag filled with some of her clothes, Alice's choice of outfits was still fairly limited. Gone were the clothes she used to wear into the Agency office, the navy slacks and Oxford button-downs and the navy jacket and black dress shoes.

Now the best Alice could do to dress for her meeting was put on her black jeans, a long-sleeved yellow T-shirt, her black fleece vest, and a pair of black waterproof rubber-soled boots from the supply room at the Factory.

She hadn't brought any clothing for the snow. She didn't have any. And when she left San Diego she had no idea she'd end up in the winter mountains. But the supply room at the Factory was like a small department store. Both Alice and her friend Marnie Stemple outfitted themselves with the kind of gear and clothing they needed, including long down coats for when they wanted to leave the unground facility and go up top, outside.

Properly weather-proofed, Alice climbed the metal steps from the Factory, pushed open the heavy door, and stepped outside into the frigid February air.

And now, once a month, never on the same date or the same day of the week, Alice made that same trek up top to find Camper waiting for her, warming up the Major's jet. It was a faster process now in the summer. Alice still wore jeans and T-shirts to their meetings, but a pair of light hikers now took the place of snow boots.

Major Zimholt's jet was a kind of luxury Alice still wasn't used to. She was twenty-six and had lived modestly her whole life. Back in San Diego, she used to live in a studio apartment and drove an eleven-year-old Honda. She bought her clothes at discount stores. Not because she couldn't afford better, but because she didn't want expensive things. That just wasn't how she was raised.

Her family of three had always lived comfortably. Alice's mother was an emergency room doctor and her father was a systems engineer. But her parents never seemed interested in having the latest of anything, in showing off in any way, in competing with what anyone around them had. Alice was the same way. She liked to live simply. Since coming to the Factory to hide, she certainly got her wish.

Now she lived in a single room on the second underground floor, with just enough space for a bed and a few other pieces of furniture, and with a bathroom smaller than the one in her old studio apartment. No kitchen. She shared a communal kitchen if she wanted to cook for herself, and otherwise ate from the cafeteria on her floor.

Marnie was still her only real friend there, although Marnie seemed to have made friends of her own over the past few months. But Alice wasn't much for socializing, even though there were hundreds of other people to choose from who lived and worked at the Factory, along with occasional outsiders who cycled in and out. So far Alice was still discovering who people were and what they did one by one as she had any reason for interacting with them.

She used to be social. She used to be friendly and outgoing. She used to be a lot of things. But a gunman had changed everything six years ago, when Alice was twenty years old and a junior in college. She watched the news of a mass shooting and somehow *knew* her parents were in that crowd. The police showed up later to confirm it.

They claimed it was just a random shooting, but Alice had a feeling about that too. She never believed their theory, even though she didn't have a good reason why. But lately, as she found out more about her parents from the files in the database at the Factory, Alice felt more certain than ever that she was right.

Her parents weren't just random people. Someone wanted Dr. Aurora Kern and Will Kern dead. Alice was going to prove it. And then hunt down the people responsible and make sure they paid, one way or another.

The jet was beginning its descent. Alice leaned back into the soft leather armchair and corralled her impatience.

She was sitting alone in the back half of the jet, the part set up like an expensive office suite with eight leather armchairs that swiveled and reclined, and glossy wooden tables set up between the pairs.

The front half of the cabin was a lounge area with two

soft leather couches that could fold out into beds. Alice was never on the jet long enough to need that, but she could imagine how much nicer that would be than some of the red-eyes she had flown in coach.

There were always fresh flowers in a vase near the front of the cabin. Today it was filled with white daisies. Alice's favorites. And there was always a meal, usually some kind of delicious lunch, served on actual china plates with real silverware.

Even if Alice still couldn't get used to all the luxury, she knew that Gina loved it. Especially the in-flight lunches. A little dose of gourmet dining to break up the stale coffee and sandwiches-on-the-run that normally fueled her day.

The jet rolled to a stop. Bruce opened the door and unfolded the short set of steps. Gina jogged up them and entered the cabin. She gave Bruce a friendly touch on the shoulder and called out a greeting to Camper, the pilot. Then she strode back to the rear of the cabin as Bruce retrieved the steps, closed the door, and Camper began taxiing to lift off again.

Gina sank into the seat across from Alice and pulled the cross-body strap of her khaki document bag up over her head. She set the bag on the seat beside her. Gina was at least ten years older than Alice, in her mid- to late-thir-ties, with shoulder-length curly brown hair she kept tugged back into a low ponytail. She wore dark athletic pants and a pale blue zip-up shirt that made it look like she had just come in from a run. Maybe she had. Gina seemed the type to work out several times a day. She was tall and fit and muscular in a way that made Alice feel puny whenever she stood beside her.

But it also gave Gina an aura of strength that made Alice feel like she could relax in the investigator's presence. As if Alice could let down her guard for at least a short time, knowing that Gina would have her back.

"We might need to start meeting every two weeks," Gina said. "A month is too long to wait."

Alice was glad to hear it. She felt cut off from people like her. She missed the energy of working around other analysts and investigators at the Agency. She loved these sessions with Gina when the two of them could brainstorm and strategize. Twice a month would be great.

Gina dug into her document bag and pulled out a stack of files that made Alice's pupils dilate. So much information. There would be photos and documents and copies of case files in there—Alice couldn't wait to dive in.

She had a stack of documents too, although not nearly that large. She brought them in an orange day pack she got from the supply room at the Factory. The pack came filled with gear for a short mountain expedition: two-liter water bladder, first aid kit, rain poncho, titanium box for food. Alice left them all in her room and filled the space with paperwork instead.

"You first," Alice said.

"Okay. Let's start with him." Gina pulled a photograph out of the file folder on top of the stack and slid it across the polished table.

Alice caught her breath. Of course she knew the man in the photo. Gina would too. He was the man who had attacked them with a knife in a bookstore back in December. The one who had stabbed Gina in the back, puncturing her lung, and then tried to kill Alice.

But Alice killed him instead.

"We knew his name from his fingerprints," Gina said. "But guess what else we know now?"

She opened the top file folder again and removed four more color photographs. Mug shots. Alice studied each of the faces.

"Know any of them?" Gina asked.

"None. I've never seen them in surveillance photos or in person." Alice looked across the table at Gina. "So who are they?"

"Part of the same brotherhood," Gina said. "A small cell operating out of LA. All of them suspected of multiple hits."

Alice returned to the first photograph of a black-haired brute named Utkin. He had worn glasses in the bookstore. Maybe because he thought they made him look studious so he could blend in better.

"Lavrev?" Alice asked. It was a name she had first

heard from Major Zimholt. According to the Major, Lavrev was a Russian oligarch who was head of the largest Russian syndicate. Major Zimholt thought it was Lavrev who hired the first assassin, a man named Danic, to come after Alice. But so far neither Alice nor Gina had found firm proof of that.

Gina was also looking into connections between Lavrev and the second assassin, Utkin. She hadn't found anything concrete as of their last meeting, but Alice assumed she must have more now. If Gina had four new photographs to lay out, it must mean she had a story to tell.

And she did.

Just not one that Alice expected or wanted.

2

Lunch was served. For the moment, nothing else mattered. At least not to Gina. She was starving.

And she was grateful for the interruption. She still wasn't sure how to introduce the topic at hand. She had rehearsed several openings: *I meant to tell you, I'm head of a new division now ... Okay, I need you to keep an open mind....*

But so far nothing felt right. She hoped she would know her opening when she found it.

Bruce the cabin steward looked distinctly like an Army Ranger to Gina. She liked the type. Not so brawny they could barely fold their arms, but solid like a chunk of marble and quick on their feet.

He set out the fancy plates and cloth napkins and water glasses for two. No wine glasses. Gina wasn't much of a drinker, and when she did indulge, beer was her liquid of choice.

She was more of a coffee junkie, and the coffee Bruce served was always excellent. Also in fancy cups, although Gina would have preferred a good tall mug.

Lunch was a Caprese salad with cold slices of mozzarella and fresh tomatoes and basil, splashed with what she could have sworn was homemade Italian dressing.

Bruce followed it with warmed eggplant sandwiches on slices of French bread with more mozzarella melted and oozing from the center.

Gina knew that Bruce didn't cook the fine meals himself—at least she assumed he didn't—but damn if she didn't feel like taking him home after these flights and installing him in her cozy little condo.

"Thanks," she told him when he finally took away their plates and returned with a full carafe of fresh coffee. Alice seemed faintly amused by the longing look Gina gave him as he walked away.

"Anyway," Alice said.

"Anyway," Gina agreed. She brushed away the crumbs from her sandwich and grabbed the top folder off the pile she had moved onto the seat beside her. She opened it again and spread the four new photos out for Alice to see.

"So what magic did you use?" Alice asked.

Gina knew her opening when she saw it.

"Funny you should say that," she said. "Let me show you something."

She pulled out a plain brown mailing envelope large enough to contain the photos. She handed it to Alice.

"Hold it up to the light," Gina said. "Can you see into it?"

Alice held up the envelope, checked it, shook her head.

Gina took the envelope back and slid the photo of Utkin, the assassin from the bookstore, into it.

"Okay, check again," Gina said.

Alice repeated the exercise. Again she shook her head. "Can't see anything."

Gina cleared her throat. She knew she should have told Alice her news months ago, but she just hadn't found the right way to do it.

But now she was committed. She could already imagine Alice's reaction. Gina had been seeing it on her fellow investigators' faces ever since her new assignment was announced back in February.

Better to start with the lights and razzle dazzle before giving Alice the punch line.

"So imagine this," Gina said. "I give this envelope to someone with this same picture inside and I ask them where this person was on a specific date and a specific time."

Alice raised her eyebrows. Gina knew she must guess where this was going.

"And this person tells me—actually, doesn't tell me, but tells one of my investigators—that inside the envelope is a picture of a man whose name is Oleg Utkin, he lives at such and such address, he's thirty-seven, all sorts of details, and at that date and time he was in a certain bookstore at this address, et cetera."

Alice gave her a skeptical look. "Okay, so ... what's the trick? Plus we already know all that."

"And then this person tells us," Gina continued, "that Oleg Utkin is there at the bookstore to kill someone named Alice Kern—"

Alice sat up straight. "No."

"Yes," Gina said, smiling. The intensity on Alice's face was just what she hoped to see. "And furthermore, he was there at the direction of someone named Simon—"

"Simon?" Alice said. "Who's Simon? We don't know any Simon yet."

Gina held up her finger. "Wait. And then my person also tells us the names of four other men—" Gina gestured to the remaining four photos. "—and gives us their names too. And they check out. Criminal records, known associates, current whereabouts. All of it. These are our guys."

"Wow," Alice whispered. She gaped at Gina with her

dark brown eyes. "I can't believe it." Then she smiled and held up her hand. "Well done!"

Gina slapped the offered hand. "Not the whole pie, but certainly a nice juicy slice."

"So who is this person?" Alice asked. "Some informant?"

"Mm, not exactly." Gina stalled by gathering the photos back into a nice neat stack. She slid them and the plain brown envelope back into their proper folder.

"Gina..." Alice was looking at her with a critical eye. "What's going on?"

"Ever heard of the Finders Division?" Gina asked.

"No. Should I?"

"I'm head of it now. It was disbanded several years ago, but I've reactivated it. Gathered all the Finders again—at least the ones who are still alive."

"What are Finders?" Alice asked.

"They ... see things. Sometimes at a distance. Sometimes even in the past. Like my friend Mrs. Byers." Gina patted the top of the folder. "She's the one who found these scum for us."

Alice slumped back into her seat. "What are you telling me? These are psychics?"

"Some of them," Gina said. "Some do what's called Far Seeing. It's actually pretty scientific—"

"Gina—"

Gina held up her hand. The one that had so recently

slapped against Alice's in celebration. "I know. I've heard it, believe me. But let me remind you of something."

Gina had come prepared. She was glad she'd thought of it. Because she had been the one to introduce Alice to the idea of another anomaly about seven months ago. Gina had to do it from her hospital bed while recovering from Utkin's knife wound to her lung.

She had given Alice a set of her own personal comic books featuring one of Gina's favorite heroines, the mighty female warrior Lenna. In the final installment of the series, Lenna returned from the dead as an avenging angel, complete with wings.

Gina didn't say it at the time, but she already knew that Alice was about to meet a real-life woman who was able to fly. Marnie Stemple. No wings on that one, but from what Gina had heard, Marnie could take off from a running start, flap her arms, and actually get herself airborne.

It was Marnie Stemple's photograph that Gina now pulled out of a separate file.

She slid it across the table to Alice.

Alice looked at it. "So?"

"So, if I had told you that night in the hospital, *Hey, Alice, you're about to meet a flier, get ready!* you would have looked at me the same way you are now. But you came around, didn't you? Because you saw her with your own eyes."

Alice took a sip of coffee. She didn't answer right away.

Gina topped off her own cup from the carafe and sat back to enjoy it while she watched Alice wrestle with the new facts.

"So you're telling me this person—Mrs..."

"Byers," Gina said.

"Byers took that envelope from you—"

"Or one like it," Gina said. "And not actually from me. I didn't want to influence any of her answers. I had one of my investigators do the interview. I watched from another room."

It was part of Gina's double-blind protocol. She had read about it in the old files she researched about the previous incarnation of the Finders Division. One person would select the targets—they might be photographs, a name on a slip of paper, coordinates to a location along with a specific time and date when something significant took place there—and then a separate interviewer who knew nothing about what was inside the envelope would ask the Finder, like Mrs. Byers, the questions.

What do you see?

What is the person's name?

What do you see that person doing?

Who else is there?

Why is this person doing what you are seeing?

A skilled interviewer could act spontaneously and go with the flow of the information. There was no set list of questions. It was a conversation with the Finder to extract as much information as possible before the trail inevitably went cold. Sometimes the Finder might talk for an hour and have a wealth of details to share, but sometimes the interviews ended quickly. The Finder just couldn't seem to latch on to anything significant.

Gina had worked with Mrs. Byers, an elegant older lady in her seventies, several times now, both in the office and out in the field. Mrs. Byers had been with her during a frightening encounter on New Year's Day that led to Gina wanting to revive the Finders Division and learn more about their extraordinary abilities.

Gina wouldn't mind enhancing those abilities in herself. But she wasn't telling anyone that. She doubted she ever would.

But she wasn't just blindly accepting everything the Finders told her. No matter how accurate some of them were. Even Mrs. Byers wasn't a hundred percent on every fact. But she had given Gina so much information now that never could have come out another way, Gina had come to rely on her more and more.

And to keep giving her brown paper envelopes containing clues to some of the Agency's long list of unsolved or stalled cases.

In the past six months, Gina had been able to resurrect at least a dozen cases that had been sitting untouched in metal file cabinets for years.

Her fellow investigators might think the Finders Division was full of oddballs, but the oddballs were getting it done.

Alice set down her coffee cup. She still slouched back in her seat. Gina recognized the body language. Alice was resistant. Gina needed to fix that before she went any further.

"There's science behind it," she said. "Real science. Out of the former USSR, believe it or not. They took it seriously there back in the sixties, and finally the US started catching up." She leaned forward, closing the distance toward the reluctant Alice. "I know it sounds fringe. But Marnie is real. There are other strange things in this world that are true. Just ... hear me out."

Was it too soon? Or was this the right time? Gina had to go with her gut.

She thumbed through the pile of file folders beside her and pulled out another plain brown envelope.

Alice wasn't going to like it. But like it or not, she would have to take it.

"Last week I had my interviewer give this one to Mrs. Byers. Open it."

Alice tore open the sealed flap of the mailing envelope and peered inside. She pulled out the single sheet of paper containing a series of typewritten numbers.

"The top set are coordinates," Gina said. "That's how

we identify locations. We don't name them. And the bottom numbers..."

But Alice was already staring at them. Gina didn't have to tell her.

It was the date of Alice's parents' murder. The coordinates were of the location where it happened.

Alice raised her gaze to Gina. She looked hurt, or confused, or maybe even defeated. None of those were the reactions Gina wanted.

Alice asked quietly, "Why?"

Gina needed to turn this around. Get it back on track. Get Alice to see that what Gina did was good.

"Because the Finders know things," Gina said. "They just do. And if I didn't use them, I'd be doing this investigation with one arm tied behind my back."

Alice dropped the paper on top of the envelope and pushed both of them back toward Gina. She got up from her seat. "I need a break. I have to think about this."

Gina didn't try to stop her. Maybe a break was a good idea. Let Alice take time to see that what Gina was offering her was progress. Real progress after Alice had been working on her parents' case mostly by herself for over the past year. Gina wanted to make a real contribution. And she had. Or at least, Mrs. Byers had.

Alice made her way toward the back of the plane to the bathroom. She opened the wooden door and disappeared inside. The lock snicked into place.

Gina let out a sigh. She wasn't sure if that was how she expected it to go, or whether it had gone well or not.

She didn't know anything. She was just trying. That was all she could do lately. Just throw out her line on the ocean and see what big fish she might be able to catch.

Finding the person or people behind the Kerns' murder would be an awfully huge fish. Maybe not in the scheme of things at the Agency level, but for Alice Kern. Gina wanted to help her.

As long as Alice would let her do it.

The jet's bathroom was nicer than the one Alice used to have in her apartment. Not much smaller, either. There was a walk-shower, a slatted wooden bench with plush white towels left rolled up and waiting, a porcelain sink embedded in what might be a granite counter top, and another vase of fresh flowers, this time white roses.

Alice leaned over the sink and stared at her face in the large round mirror.

Her mother's face. Aurora Kern was Filipino. Alice had her same dark brown skin, dark eyes, and long brown hair. She knew there were shapes to her features that came from her father's Germanic side. But any time Alice wanted to remember what her mother looked like, she only had to glance into a mirror.

It was tempting. So tempting. To believe in the fairy tale Gina was offering.

Alice used to believe—or at least enjoy—all sorts of fantasy and science fiction stories. She and her mother loved indulging in movie nights when they'd fill up on all sorts of heroic fantasies—movies with wizards and elves and immortals, martial arts flicks where warriors could soar through the air, land on their feet, vanquish every evil foe.

But reality came crashing down. Alice could hardly bear to remember how naïve and impressionable she used to be. It wasn't a sweet memory, it was a flaw. Maybe if she had been more worldly, tougher, she could have handled her parents' deaths without completely falling apart.

Other people lost loved ones. Alice wasn't unique. But her heart had suffered such irrevocable damage, she knew she would have to be careful all the rest of her life to hold the pieces together by their flimsy tattered remains. She was like a tightrope walker conscious of the brute force of every gust of wind.

She wanted to know. She didn't want to know. She wanted to know if it was real.

But if this Mrs. Byers was just a fortune teller, some charlatan—or not even charlatan, but just some misguided fantasist who believed in her own hype—then

Alice couldn't afford to listen to a word of it. She couldn't afford to let herself believe what wasn't true.

Because if Gina was about to tell her a name. Or give her some details of the killing that Alice hadn't found out on her own. Then that information would be inside Alice's head forever from then on. And she might be so misled she would never find the real trail again. She would never really solve her parents' murder.

But of course she wanted to know. Dear God. If it were only that simple.

Alice had never told anyone—she could hardly stand to know it herself—but in the months after her parents' death, she began a private, secret search among the various mediums in the San Diego area. People who claimed they could communicate with the dead. That they could channel them and let the deceased actually speak through them to their loved ones left behind.

Alice looked at their websites. Read their testimonials. Researched complaints against them. Looked for any sign that even one of them could be trusted. That the purported medium wasn't just taking advantage of people in grief.

And finally Alice chose one. Not very scientifically. She liked the woman's picture. The soft look in her eyes. Her sympathetic face. She looked kind and motherly. Alice found herself staring at the woman's picture day after day, and then finally she found the courage to schedule an appointment.

The experience was surreal.

The woman looked exactly like her picture. No makeup, slightly homely, but with a kindness that came through her gaze.

The woman, Claudine, reached out both her hands to take Alice's between them. Her touch was warm and comforting. Alice was afraid she might start crying just because of that. She had been resisting all the people around her who constantly offered their condolences and asked if she was all right. Of course she wasn't all right. But she always put up a brave front and got rid of the well-wisher as soon as possible. She stood back when they came in for a hug. She didn't want to be held. What she wanted was for none of it to have ever happened.

But Claudine was a stranger, and somehow her warmth felt right to accept. Alice let Claudine lead her into the small and tidy house, into a small dining room with an old-fashioned polished table. There were already two water glasses sitting on coasters in front of two facing chairs. Alice sat on the near one and Claudine went around the table to sit across from her.

Alice's heart was racing. Was she doing the right thing? What would her parents think of this? Would they try to make her stop, would they tell her she was being foolish?

She could imagine coming here with her mother. Maybe as a Mother's Day gift or a birthday present. A fun mother-daughter outing, just something different, a lark, just to see what a medium actually did.

Instead Alice sat alone, heart leaping, her breath feeling hard and ragged in her throat.

"Just relax, dear," Claudine told her. She was in her sixties, maybe, short and a little overweight, with frizzy gray hair held back from her face with a black stretchy hairband.

"I've never done this before," Alice said.

"It's all right," Claudine said. "Nothing to be afraid of."

Claudine reached across the table, inviting Alice to do the same. The surface was wide enough that their fingers barely met.

Alice wondered why Claudine did the session in here, rather than somewhere where she could sit closer to her client. But Alice continued lengthening her arms across the table, anxious now to find even the slightest grip so Claudine wouldn't let go.

"Thank you," Claudine said. "That's all." She retracted her arms and folded her hands together in front of her on top of the table. Alice reluctantly retracted her arms too and placed her hands on her lap.

The form Alice filled out to schedule the appointment asked only for her first name. No last name, no details about who she wanted to contact. Alice appreciated that. It meant Claudine couldn't look her up ahead of time.

Payment was in cash at the appointment, so Claudine didn't have Alice's credit card information either. It seemed like a clean system.

Alice could have used a fake name, and she almost did, but she decided if she was going to do this, she should do it all the way. Not lie, but also not offer any information during her session. Just let Claudine "read her" and see if she could channel the deceased persons Alice was seeking.

"Let me look at you, dear," Claudine said. Her gaze was still soft, just like in her picture on her website, but now it felt penetrating as she stared into Alice's eyes.

Alice wanted to look away. She might not have minded it when she was younger, but after everything that had happened, she realized she felt very sensitive about being seen.

But if she was going to do this, she should do it. Alice kept her gaze steady on Claudine's for what felt like five minutes straight.

Then finally Claudine whispered, "Thank you," and she closed her eyes and began breathing deeply.

Alice sat through several long, tense minutes, again wondering whether she should have ever come here. The price was reasonable—just two hundred dollars, where some other mediums charged five hundred or more—and

Claudine seemed normal and down to earth, but this was still so far out of Alice's comfort range it was hard to stay in the high-backed wooden chair and not bolt for the front door.

Then Claudine's voice came softly again, saying, "They passed not long ago." She wrinkled her brow. "Oh, I'm so sorry. How tragic. You must have been devastated."

Alice pressed her lips together. She would not speak. If this was a trick, it was the easiest one to see. Claudine would say something general—*How tragic. How sad*—and the grieving person would spill their guts and maybe even share some of the details of what made the death so awful.

"Your mother is here," Claudine said. The medium raised her hand into the air and stroked it downward a few times, as if Aurora Kern herself might be trying to stroke Alice's hair. It was a gesture Alice recognized.

Alice caught the sound that wanted to erupt from her throat. She swallowed it down hard before it could turn into a sob. She clenched her hands together on her lap. She sat upright and as still as possible. If this was a trick, she wasn't falling for it.

"And your father," Claudine said.

Maybe she did research Alice after all. Maybe she had some way of locking into the location of Alice's computer when she made the appointment. Then it would be easy to find the newspaper articles about the shooting. They went on and on for months.

"He's showing me ... he's showing me..." Claudine wrinkled her brow again. "It's an egg timer. Does that mean anything to you?"

Alice covered her mouth with her hand. Claudine's eyes were still closed. Alice tried to keep it together.

But yes, she recognized an egg timer. It was part of a game she played with her father. Name as many of X as you can in two minutes. Capital cities, names of rivers, songs that begin with *S*, foods that begin with *M*—it could be anything. Just for the fun and speed of it. To see who could win by naming more.

Sometimes they wrote their answers down, sometimes they shouted them out at each other, keeping track by counting on their fingers. Either of them could call for the game at any time—during commercials, just before guests were about to arrive for a party, first thing in the morning before her father had had his coffee—the more inconvenient, the better. Because the rule was you couldn't refuse. Will Kern used that to his advantage when Alice was anxious to leave the house to go out with her friends. Her father would pull out the egg timer, and Alice would have to stop and play. She pretended to be annoyed, but the truth was she loved it. It was their tradition, carried over from her childhood, all the way up until Will Kern died. Alice could remember playing it with him when she stopped by the house to visit her parents just a few weeks before the shooting.

Name dogs from movies. Go.

Lassie, Air Bud, Hundred and One Dalmations—

That's the name of the movie, not the dog!

—Benji, Marley, White Fang—

"Alice?" Claudine said quietly. "Does an egg timer mean anything to you?"

Alice couldn't resist. "Y-yes."

Claudine smiled. "Good. And your mother is here. She says she loves you…"

And now Alice was crying, and from then on it only got worse.

When the session was over, Alice paid Claudine her two hundred dollars and added a twenty dollar tip.

She left Claudine's house with red, swollen eyes and an ache in her chest that felt even more painful than when she arrived.

It was easy to start picking apart everything Claudine said, and everything Alice confirmed. Easy to see how Alice might have been led from one answer to another, feeling her out, reading her, telling her what she wanted to hear.

Except for the egg timer.

That. No one could have found that in an article about the killing, or in any internet search about Alice Kern. The information had to have come from another source.

Alice mulled over the session detail by detail for days and weeks afterward.

Was it true? Was any of it true?

And even if it was, what had she really learned?

Claudine, speaking on behalf of Will and Aurora Kern, assured Alice over and over how much they loved her.

Yes, it hurt like a stab wound to her heart to hear it said. Alice sobbed. All her plans about being stoic and unreadable fell apart so quickly, she wondered why she thought she would be able to do it at all.

She was a wreck. The session felt as if all it did was open Alice's barely-closed wounds. She shut herself away. Didn't answer her phone, texts, emails, ignored knocking and sometimes pounding on her door.

When the commotion became too much, she drove to the beach and walked for hours.

So no, it hadn't helped her at all. In some ways it had made her grief far worse than before. Because now all she wanted to do was go back to Claudine's house and pay her two hundred dollars a day just to hear words that any medium could fake if she wanted to.

We miss you. We love you. We're so proud of you.

And now Gina. Offering something that might be equally alluring and maybe equally untrue.

But Marnie Stemple is real.

Just like the egg timer was real.

Alice gripped the edges of the sink and leaned forward and rested the top of her head against the cold mirror. When she pulled away there was a smudge where she would normally look for her mother's eyes staring out through hers.

Alice sank onto the slatted wooden bench across from the shower. She leaned back against the wall and caught her breath. She knew what she had to do, she just needed another few minutes. Two minutes, to be exact.

Set the egg timer. Two minutes to name all the reasons why you don't want to do this. Go.

Because it might be fake. It might be real. I might learn more than I'm ready to know. I might have to hear about their last minutes. I don't want to know. Were they afraid? Were they in pain? Would Gina's Finder be able to tell me? Could I stop her from telling me? She's not even here. It's already done.

What would my father do now? What would my mother do, if I was the one who had been shot? Would they want the details? Or would they rather let me go in peace?

There is no peace. There won't be. Not until I know the reason they were killed.

Dammit, don't be a coward. Go out there and fight.

Alice stood from the bench and went back to the sink. She turned on the faucet and splashed cold water against her face. She patted it dry with the soft white towel. She leaned over and smelled the white roses in the vase. Stalling, but only because she had already made up her mind. She could afford to take a moment to smell the roses.

She unlocked the door and made her way back along the carpeted floor to her fancy seat. Gina was enjoying a slice of some kind of chocolate cake on a clear glass plate.

Alice sat across from her and held out her hand for the envelope again. Gina patted her mouth with her cloth napkin and held up her finger for Alice to wait.

"I have the transcript," Gina said. "Of the whole interview. You can read it, or I'll summarize."

"Tell me again," Alice said. "Why should I think this is real?"

"Because I'm the only one who knew what was on that paper inside the envelope," Gina said. "The interviewer and Mrs. Byers went in blind. No one read her the coordinates or the date. She didn't touch the envelope. No one opened it. The interviewer placed it on the table in front of her, and Mrs. Byers just looked at it."

"And then..."

Gina finished a sip of coffee. "And then she started telling the interviewer what she saw at that place on that date. I'll be honest, parts of it are very rough. You might not need to know everything. Like I said, I have the transcript if you want it—"

"Summarize," Alice said.

She hated to feel cowardly, but she had already had her heart beaten to a bloody pulp. She trusted Gina to extract the pertinent information for the case, while sparing Alice the worst of her pain.

"Bottom line, you were right," Gina said. "The targets were Will and Aurora Kern."

Alice sucked in a breath. She wanted to know it and she didn't. But really, hadn't she known it all along? Not with any proof, just a feeling. She couldn't even say why she knew it back when she was twenty. She was still just a child. She didn't know any of the things she knew now after working for the Agency for the past year. But Alice couldn't pretend to be surprised. So she nodded and waited for more.

"We already know the shooter's name. But Mrs. Byers gave us that again. She knew a lot about his preparations for the day. I can extract that from the transcript it you want—"

"No," Alice said. "Just go on. Who hired him? Did Mrs. Byers know?"

"A first name," Gina said. "Apparently that's all the shooter knew."

Alice had a feeling. She blurted out the name.

"Simon."

Gina nodded. "Whoever that bastard is. I'm sorry, but Mrs. Byers couldn't tell us any more about him. I think it's because he was careful the shooter didn't know any more either."

Alice felt weary. And heavy with a fresh new burden.

As if she finally opened a door and found a boulder now barring her way. She couldn't lift it, she couldn't go around it or through it. She could only stare at it and wonder what on earth she was supposed to do next.

"So how does this work?" Alice asked. "Is it a dead end? Or is there some other way now to find out who Simon is?"

"We'll find out," Gina promised. "Remember those four new pictures I showed you. They work for Simon too. We'll keep digging. We'll find him."

Alice brought her hand to her face. She covered her mouth and turned to stare out the window. The sky was light blue and clotted with clouds. She wished now she hadn't eaten any of the lunch. It sat like a brick inside her belly. She wanted to go home.

Home home. Not back to the Factory. Not even back to her little studio apartment in San Diego.

Home to the place that she sold, the place where she grew up. Home to her bedroom, decorated in green and white and overstuffed with books and games and the models she and her father had built together from kits. There was an airplane that took them weeks to figure out. But everything worked and the moving parts moved: propeller, doors, wing flaps, wheels.

It was all packed away. In some storage unit Alice paid for every year. She hadn't been back to look through it since she put the lock on the door and drove away.

She couldn't go back. She could only go forward. That was the truth, as bedrock solid as anything she knew.

Alice turned back to Gina. "Okay. Then we find out who Simon is. Good work, Gina. I mean it."

"I'm sorry," Gina said.

"For what?"

"Maybe I should have asked you first."

Alice shook her head. "I would have said no. And you're right, we'd still be stuck back where we were. At least we've moved forward. I appreciate that."

Gina studied her for a moment. Alice gave her a shrug and her best attempt at a smile.

"None of this is fun," Alice said. "It never will be. You can't be afraid to tell me things I probably don't want to hear."

Gina nodded. "Okay. Got it. But I meant what I said before. I think we should start meeting every two weeks."

"Do they ... do they ever talk about me coming back?" Alice asked.

"They do," Gina said. "*I* do. But we still don't think it's safe. Not yet. Give us time. You're a good analyst. We could use you back."

Alice hadn't really expected anything different. Nothing had really changed. If she had been a threat to someone back in December, then she still was. It was why she and Gina were having this conversation high among the clouds rather than at the Agency amid the bustle of investigations.

Alice felt a slight tilt in the pit of her stomach. Camper must be starting another descent. They couldn't hide up here forever. Gina had work to do. So did Alice.

They traded their stacks of files and both stowed them away, Gina in her khaki document bag and Alice in her orange day pack.

"If it was me," Gina said, "I wouldn't read transcript. But I gave it to you anyway. It's your decision."

Alice nodded. She didn't answer. She wasn't sure what she was going to do or what she would say.

When the jet came to a stop on the private runway, Gina pulled out her service weapon and waited at the door with Bruce. But no one was waiting to attack. Maybe no one ever would. Maybe all of these precautions were unnecessary. But four assassins had tried to kill Alice, one of them had stabbed Gina, and someone else had tried to shoot her not long after. It was the nature of precautions to feel unnecessary—until they were. For now, none of them were interested in letting down their guard.

As soon as Gina was safely off, Camper wheeled the jet around and took off again.

Alice had noticed before that it never needed refueling. She knew nothing about jets. Maybe they could fly a whole day on one tank of gas. She had enough things to try to know without adding that one.

As she stared out the window at the slow, puffy clouds, Alice could feel the tightness in her chest gradually ease.

She laid her hand on top of the orange daypack. There were enough documents in there to keep her occupied reading for days. And once she started cross-referencing some of the names with the files in the Factory database, she might have whole new vistas to explore by the end of the week.

And then maybe Gina would take some of that information and hide it in a plain brown envelope. And maybe Mrs. Byers or one of the other Finders would tell them details they could never expect.

If this was the way it was going to be from now on, maybe Alice should just accept it and not fight it in the least.

There were moments even now when she regretted not going back to see Claudine. Not asking for more, give me more, tell me more.

Maybe her mother would reach out with some private memory of her own. Something that only she and Alice had shared.

Maybe Alice's father would move beyond mentioning just the egg timer, and would tell Alice some truth that she needed to know.

Maybe maybe maybe.

Alice had had enough of maybes. She needed action and facts and truth. She needed to know she was doing what she could, every day, to find out why her parents were gone.

It didn't take a medium to tell Alice her parents loved her and missed her. Alice knew it. Just as they would have known it if she were the one who died.

But if Claudine or Mrs. Byers or someone else could tell Alice what was hiding behind that huge boulder in her way, then she wanted to hear it. She wanted to know it. She was ready.

Simon. Who are you, Simon? I'm going to find you, Simon. I'm going to get you.

Back when Alice was young, maybe nine or ten, she had a lesson one night at the dojo that she never forgot.

It was with her Uncle Edilmark, who was ten years older than Alice's mother and had been born in the Philippines before the family emigrated to America. The other brother, Alice's Uncle Condring, was two years older than that. They were both in their late forties then, about the age Alice's mother was when she was killed, and they were strong and serious and funny at times, and much alike and yet distinctly different.

Uncle Edilmark had the slighter build of the two. He looked more like Alice's mother than the other brother. He kept his thick brown hair long, in a ponytail down his back, like the warriors in martial arts films. He was fast and nimble. His hands could move in a blur, like Bruce

Lee's. Watching him spar with the black belts was like watching a cheetah go after gazelles.

Uncle Condring was taller than his other two siblings, and also stocky and solid and practically immovable. He was a stockbroker by day, dojo owner and instructor by night, so he kept his graying hair cut short and corporate-looking for his bosses and clients. Alice was always surprised by how natural he looked in both his business suits and in the heavy black cotton pants and jacket that made up the *gi* he wore in the dojo.

Both of her uncles taught young Alice how to fight in the Filipino style they had learned when they were boys. Then Alice's mother taught her her own techniques for taking down bigger opponents like Alice's uncles.

Alice's mother was sneaky and scrappy. Alice always liked her lessons best.

But the lesson from Uncle Edilmark made a different kind of impression on Alice. One she still applied at times like these when she was feeling overwhelmed and frustrated and lost.

She was working with Uncle Edilmark on improving her blocks against punches to her face. She could react swiftly, get her arm into position in time to deflect the blow, but Alice still couldn't help flinching away. Jerking her head back. She didn't trust her block enough to calmly stand her ground.

Uncle Edilmark identified the problem. He said, "You

only think of being attacked. You are thinking what they want to do to you. But you should think of what *you* are doing to *them*."

He told her to see it only from her own side. "Someone has activated you. Someone has woken you up. Now *you* are doing a thing." He pulled her arm up into position. Her fist was tight, ready for the block. "They shouldn't have done it," her uncle said. "Now they must face you. Believe in your power, Alice. *You* are doing a thing."

He backed away, into position, and threw a punch toward her face again.

Alice glared back at him as she raised her forearm into the block. And this time she leaned in. She went for it. She pushed him back with the force of her block. Even though she was only a small girl defending against the punch from a grown man. *She* was doing a thing.

As Camper continued his descent over the Wasatch Mountains, down toward the Factory's hidden airport, Alice could feel the change inside her body. A tilt. A new angle. And she could feel the change in her mind.

She had been on the defensive for over six years now. Reeling. Reacting. Holding so tightly to keeping herself together.

Wanting to know the truth—and afraid of knowing the truth. Why had the two people who meant everything to her been taken away? *Why?* It was a quest she realized now she was afraid of. It was the punch aiming at her face. She would block it because that was what she was trained to do. But she was afraid of it. She still wanted to jerk her head away.

No, *I'm* doing a thing.

Activated. Awakened. Stepping into it. Pushing back.

Pushing, defending, then fighting with all of her skill and might. Not just cowering away from the blows. She had been doing that for too long. Hiding behind her research. Seeking, but then hiding from knowing too much.

None of it on purpose, none of it even punching through to her awareness. It was only now, staring out the jet window to the masses of yellow and purple wildflowers growing all along the hillsides down below, that Alice was willing to see with fresh eyes the change in the seasons. The new growth. The way that winter gave in to the force of a mountain summer. Even up this high in the Wasatch Mountains, where spring had been short and late and barely noticeable until late June, the flowers did come. The snow did melt. The sun did shine, no matter what.

She could move forward. Change. Arise.

Someone has activated you. Someone has woken you up. Now you are doing a thing. They shouldn't have done it. Now they must face you.

They must face her. The four men in Gina's files.

Simon, whoever he was. Everyone who was responsible. Every last one of them.

Alice sat up straight. She could feel the strength flowing back into her limbs.

She wasn't afraid of the truth anymore. She would know it all.

She would get back on the mat and fight.

And one day she was going to make this right.

YOU WILL FIND MORE stories about Alice Kern and Gina Firenzi in the books DOVE SEASON, FINDER, SEEKER, and BELIEVER, part of the Dove Season Universe by Robin Brande.

SECOND LIFE

INTRODUCTION

Theoretical physicist Dr. Angela Corliss survived a wild and uncontrollable alien encounter at a gathering of scientists in the remote mountains of Colorado.

Now she is on the run.

But a mysterious stranger has asked to meet her. He claims he has been using her invention for years.

Years in the past ... and maybe even years in the future. No matter how impossible that sounds.

A tale of time loops and second chances, and the unshakable power of love.

1

____

Your hair is a snarled mass of gray. Your clothes are rumpled. You've barely slept. You look exhausted.

"Not at my best," you warned me. "I'll look so dowdy. Even older than I am." But all I see is a beautiful woman standing before me. The lines and creases on your face are precious to me. Your eyes take me in with that curiosity you bring to everything in your life: Who is this man? Why does he want to meet me?

And what is this place?

We stand in the hangar of the Factory, four of us: You and me and my friends Kirsten Simmens and Fritz Zimholt, who owns this facility.

You're unsure. You're still bundled up against the cold. Outside, the Wasatch mountains of Utah are covered in a record depth of snow. Inside, underground, we're warm and protected. But all of this is new to you. So you still wear your green ski coat. But you took off your gloves. You're not wearing a ring. I knew you wouldn't, but your finger looks so bare without it. It catches my eye.

There are people moving about, tending to their work on the various aircraft down here, pilots and mechanics and at least fifty personnel, and you take it all in with your curious gaze.

Then you turn your eyes back to me.

You don't remember me. There's no reason you should. We hatched this meeting years ago. This date, this place, this aftermath of what you just experienced in the mountains of Colorado.

But I have been busy all this time, seeding myself along your path over the last few years. I came to several of your conferences. We never spoke. But I was the tall black man out in the crowd nodding as you explained your theories. I wasn't like your colleagues, scowling at your brilliant ideas.

I was the man in the grocery store in Madison, Wisconsin a few times, reaching for something off a high shelf for you that you couldn't quite reach yourself.

That self-conscious laugh. "Thanks." Always that genuine smile. How I loved you.

So many times we could have met along this time line, but I had to hold back. We always knew it had to be right.

It had to be like this, in this exact moment, or nothing would work the way we wanted it to.

I told you in the beginning, the first time we met, what my strategy was. "I'm going to be nice to you."

That took you by surprise. As if no one had ever tried that before. But you settled right into it. You softened and leaned back. You let me love you sooner than you might otherwise. I'm a maker by nature, and this was a love worth making.

Not just once, but again. As many times as I'm allowed.

We talked about your theory that every choice exists, and every choice is made. Which means there are time-lines when we never meet. Others where we meet and don't connect.

Unacceptable, sweetheart, as I've told you.

So even though this was meant to be a clean choice, completely unweighted on either side, I'll admit I have done a few things to skew it.

Not so much that I worry I've ruined your chance at a fresh loop of time, but enough to maybe help us along.

So I have been that face in the crowd, that approving nod, that friendly stranger who helped you for a moment and moved on. I figured it would create echoes. A subtle familiarity so that today, in this moment, you would look at me the way you are, wondering if you know me.

"Dr. Corliss," I say, extending my hand. "Reggie Swan. So good to meet you."

"Angela, please." That smile I know so well, even though you look worn to the bone. It's been a hard, hard night for you.

You knew it would be. You already did it once in your other life. But you said you had to do it again. Do it right. Last time you left early. Last time, you told me, you were a coward. This time you were going to stay and learn all of it.

We shake hands. This hand of yours that I've held tenderly thousands of times. The knuckles I have raised to my lips to kiss. "Courtly," you told me once. That's right, ma'am. You deserve every formal demonstration of love.

How did I find you the first time? My alien friend RayJay showed me the key. Searching with my heart across time and space, not knowing who I was supposed to be looking for, but just letting my time map—my heart map—lock onto you.

Heart, mind, body and soul. Everything I could ever want from a love.

And clearly my intellectual superior, even though you still refuse to admit it. I might be able to make nearly anything I set my hand to, but I needed your mind to help me figure out the missing parts.

Your Pure Dark Energy. I couldn't have made any of this without you. Nothing in this hangar. All of these experimental aircraft, the spacecraft, are here because of you.

There are so many more things I need to make, and I need you still. Again. But over here in a second time loop. It's your theory, not mine: how to take the gains of the past several years and add to them now with new knowledge, new ideas. And that way go further.

You had a strange way of explaining it. Like a person dying and coming back into their already existing body. Reincarnating in place.

"That way you don't have to waste time being a baby and a teenager and going through all that again," you said. "You bank the gains. But you start over and let it take you further. Higher."

"Why can't we just go on the way we are?" I asked you. Stopping, starting over—it made no sense. And I resisted having to lose you, even temporarily.

"Because we both already took certain paths," you said. "We already used up a bunch of years. I need a fresh loop. Start someplace different. You have to trust me on this."

The old you made herself an expert on time loops. This new you is still skeptical about them. You told me that was the way.

"We all get too entrenched in our ways of habitual thinking," you said. "The only way forward is to break free."

Reincarnate in place. Stop, begin again, find each other again.

And so here we are, at last. I tell you a little about this place, the Factory. I talk to you as if I don't know you. As if you haven't been my wife for ten years. I want to kiss you. Hold you. The others don't know, Fritz and Kirsten. Not in this timeline. Think how shocked they would be if I just reached for you now and brought us both back where we belong.

You yawn. You can't help it. You cover your mouth and look embarrassed.

"You must be bushed," I say. "And here I am talking."

"I just need a short rest," you say. "But then I want to hear everything. Of course. I need to know all of this."

I offer to show you to your room. It's down two floors, deeper underground, down where Fritz keeps the guest quarters for people like me passing through.

But I'm not just passing through this time. I'll be staying a good long while. You couldn't tear me away.

I wish I could hold your hand as we descend the stairs. I wish I could put my arm around you and pull you in close against my hip, the way we liked to be. We fit perfectly together. We always have.

"Oh, I do remember," you say suddenly as we round the corner and head toward your room.

You stop in the hallway and look up at me. I don't

know what to say. What to do. This wasn't how we planned.

"You told me you're an Orioles fan," you say. And I let out a surprised laugh.

"I never said that."

You squint your beautiful, intelligent eyes at me and give me that smile I'm never tired of.

"Then something," you say. "I remember you from somewhere." You yawn again. "I'll think of it. I just need to sleep."

I leave you at your room. I show you how to make an imprint of your hand on the panel inset in the door. "It'll open just for you." *And anyone else you want to let in.* I think it but don't say it. But I would give a million dollars to come in with you right now.

We've been separated too long. You said it had to be that way so your mind would let you forget.

I give you a little bow. "Good night, then."

You smile. I almost expect you to say *How courtly,* but you don't.

I have to leave you and take my aching heart back up the stairs.

2

I fell asleep so hard and so fast, you would think someone beaned me over the head.

The room they gave me is sparse, easy on the eyes and nerves. I liked the country cabin effect of Dr. Adam Proul's mountain mansion, but right now seeing anything made of pine or oak wouldn't soothe me in the least. The white and gray room, the concrete walls, the sleek tile in the bathroom—everything looks modern and clean. A fresh start.

I fell asleep in my clothes. No idea how long I was out. I start the coffeepot on the bedside table and undress to go take a shower. The hot water feels like medicine. I wash my skin, my hair. I let the events of the past few days glide down the drain. That was then. This is now. All of that is over.

This place could be my place. All the activity, the technology, the *ideas*—as exhausted as I was when I first arrived, I felt a thrill through my veins. An energy I haven't found other places—even at Dr. Proul's conference. That was a different feeling all together. This—this feels like a plausible future for me.

There's something wickedly invigorating about being around sharp, elevated minds. The kind of people who not only accept the science I've been doing, but who *want* it. Want more of it.

And what of Reggie Swan? The man who asked Kirsten to look for me and pluck me out of that equally elevated crowd.

You have a feeling about people. The way I think animals know. This one hits ... this one loves ... this one will feed me and take me in. I saw it with my neighbor once, how a feral kitten came up to him and rubbed against his leg, no doubt ready to bolt at the first sign it had misjudged the man's character.

But the kitten was right to trust him. Peter and his wife took her in, bathed her, fed her, loved her for five perfect days, and then the kitten slipped away in the night, hid inside their bathroom vanity, and died there as she must have known she was about to do.

The vet said she wasn't a kitten at all, she was probably two years old already, based on her teeth, but she was so undernourished she never grew. On top of that, her little body was riddled with parasites. She was so sick and emaciated, she must have been right on the verge of starving that day she ran to Peter for help. Five perfect days. Probably the only days of her life that she felt safe and loved.

You get a sense about people. Kind, unkind. Nourishing or draining. Worth your time, not.

The people here seem good. I already felt fine about Kirsten Simmens, even though she lied to me. I get that it was necessary. Doesn't change who she is, deep down. At a conference I once heard a psychotherapist describe people's habitual behaviors as *characterological*. We are who we are. The liar lies. In their minds, it works. They will rarely feel motivated to change into someone honest. Honesty is for suckers.

But sometimes even honest people have to take another course. Some circumstance makes it feel like the only sensible option. Like that party game of asking people if it's ever all right to lie. For some people, it's black and white: *No, never.*

"So if there's a maniac in your house who wants to harm some member of your family, and that person—your father or mother or child—is hiding in a closet, and the maniac demands to know where your loved one is—do you have to tell the truth?"

Silence. Not so clear after all.

Sometimes good people, honest people, lie. But usually the behavior is brief. They can't sustain it. We are who we are.

Fritz Zimholt? I feel fine about him. He has a calm way about him. Steady at the helm. He's obviously ambitious enough to create this whole facility and staff it with so many talented people, but I've met my share of visionaries over the years who thought they were so brilliant they had the right to climb over anybody and anything on their way to the top. There's a kind of sickness that was always there. *Characterological.* Some people get power and they can't wait to use it to hurt people. To dominate.

Fritz Zimholt doesn't strike me as that kind at all. If he did, I'd already be gone, even if I knew he had unlocked all the secrets to the universe. Not everybody agrees with me, but knowledge isn't worth your soul. You still have to live with yourself. You have to know your limits.

And that takes me back to Reggie Swan.

I can see a starving kitty running up to that man. He just exudes safety and kindness. And to be both intelligent and competent on top of it—I'll admit when he was walking me down to my room last night my eyes strayed more than once to that wedding ring on his finger. Some woman is awfully lucky.

Which isn't normally the way I think. It's been *years*

since I thought that way. The last time was probably in my thirties. No doubt some kind of hormonal prompting at the time from a body reminding me that if I wanted to have children, I'd better get after it. But the feeling passed, the colleague moved away, and I have never lacked a moment's worth of something to fill my time.

I know plenty of scientists, men and women, who have had to make the choice. Work suffers when there's a family wanting your attention. We all know it. But the lure is there. The temptation.

If you're lucky, like me, you don't have a real opportunity to choose. Makes it easy.

And then you get old. You make your discoveries. You find satisfaction—deep satisfaction—in what your mind can actually accomplish.

And maybe some day you find out some stranger has actually used your ideas to make incredible things. And he wants to show you. And suddenly you find yourself in a strange place among strangers, feeling like this is exactly where you want to be. Where you would have chosen to be if you could have mapped it out yourself.

I've always had a hard time, scientifically, making up my mind about coincidence.

But there's still a thread of faith inside me, thin and deeply buried though it sometimes feels. The faith of a girl who saw her father healed by a preacher. The faith of a grown woman who had alien power flowing through her hands just a few nights ago that allowed her to bring a man back to life.

We don't know everything. None of us. Maybe we're not supposed to.

3

————————————

I'm in the hangar, talking to one of the mechanics, when I finally catch sight of you again. You've come up to find me, I think. I hope. Here I've been, waiting to be found.

You're in a worn pair of jeans and a rose-colored sweater. Your wavy gray hair looks damp from a shower. You look fantastic. It wouldn't be proper for me to say so.

"Afternoon," I say.

You laugh. "Is it?" You brush a strand of hair away from your left eye.

You polish up nicely. I've seen it so many times before. All you need is a good night's sleep, some good food, some good conversation—something invigorating to activate your busy mind—and your whole being seems to plump right up like a raisin reverting to a grape.

You used to be able to go for a whole week on very little sleep, but then it always caught up with you.

I'd notice the way your lids sloped so heavily over your eyes, the blinks coming slower and slower, and I'd cut off whatever we were talking about right in an instant and escort you to our bed.

Sometimes, especially if we were right in the middle of the juiciest of *What-if* science conversations, you'd protest mightily. But there was no arguing with me when it came to taking care of my wife.

"You'll thank me tomorrow," I'd say, knowing you probably wouldn't—you hated to suspend any fascinating talk—but I couldn't have your exhaustion on my conscience. You always knew I had your best interest at heart.

But you seem lively enough now. Restored. And I know, true to form, you're full of all sorts of questions.

Also true to form, you ask the hardest one first.

"Tell me about this time loop," you say, and when you notice even the smallest hesitation, you add, "Kirsten already mentioned it." As if to say, *Don't even think about trying to get out of this.*

But that isn't my hesitation. Lord knows I've thought how to tell you in multiple ways, long and short, intricate and simple. It's just that as of this moment, I still don't know which is best. It feels too important to just toss off any care and say whatever comes out of my mouth first.

So I stall a bit. "Let me show you first what we've made, thanks to you."

If we were both younger, you might roll your eyes. Instead you give me a withering look, but you do go along with it. Because I know you're curious about *everything*. And what's in this hangar must be at least in the top five of that list.

I show you the current generation of pods. Not all of them are here right now. Some—a good dozen—are out in the cold mountain wind being put through their paces by the various test pilots. But there are still hundreds of pods sitting in neat rows on the clean concrete floor, lined up like so many beads on a string.

The top halves of the pods are transparent, allowing the pilots maximum visibility in all directions. The bottom halves are a dull opaque gray. The insides are a soft rose-gold color. Very soothing on the eyes.

The pods are made of a material not found here on Earth. Not in its raw state. I had to learn to duplicate it from the sample spacecraft flown here by my alien friends RayJay, Mit, and Linus. They came here for a just a few short years to share some of their technology with a few humans, like me.

It's an honor I treasure with all of my heart. One that you treasured too, once I brought you in on the project.

"I feel as if I know them," you told me more than once, back then. "I wish I could have met them."

You did meet them. Or at least they met you. You just didn't remember. You weren't supposed to.

Now, in this life, here you are stepping up to one of the pods for the very first time, examining it.

"These are all single-seaters," I tell you. "We have a few doubles, and we're working on some team transports that will hold four or five pods at a time."

You run your hand over the top of the nearest pod. I know what it feels like: warm. Skin warmth. People notice that.

You pull your hand back for a moment, as if you don't quite believe it, then press your palm against the sphere again, harder.

"This isn't normal metal," you say.

"No." I wait. You like to figure things out for yourself.

"It almost feels..." You look up at me. Wanting to see my answer with your eyes. "...alive."

"It is," I say.

"Not a machine," you say.

"No. Not the way we think of one."

"A living entity."

I nod.

You blow out a soft breath. You turn back to the pod and crouch down to run your hand along the exterior. You peer inside the transparent domed lid to the soft golden-rose interior.

"Remarkable," you whisper. "Reggie."

When you turn back to me, your eyes are sparkling with wonder. Maybe even a little wet, the way they'd sometimes get when your mind took in some expansive truth.

Then you slowly stand back up, facing me. You cross your arms over your chest and tuck your hands underneath your armpits. I wonder if you're cold. The hangar isn't freezing, but it isn't exactly balmy. Normally I would warm your hands between my own. Instead I stand this close to you, pretending it doesn't matter. Pretending to be casual as I wait for your inevitable questions. I wonder which ones you'll ask first.

"Kirsten said you've been using my Pure Dark Energy for ten years."

"I have."

You shake your head and give a half-hearted smile. "I wish I'd known. I feel like I've been out in the wilderness all this time. I didn't know anyone even cared."

"It's complicated," I say. "Believe me, I would have loved to tell you."

I did tell you. I did love you. These pods brought us together.

"Tell me about the time loop."

"Also complicated," I say. "As you might imagine."

You let out another breath. Like you're steeling yourself to hear it. Like you're gathering your brain power to absorb it.

But I vowed I wouldn't tell you too much. You wanted this chance to be clean.

"I got as far as I could on my own," I tell you. I hate to lie to you, but the truth is too sticky. Not clean at all. You made me promise.

"Ten years ago, Kirsten said. And also ... ten years from now?" You look up at me with your beautiful green eyes, ready to hear the full, amazing story.

"There abouts," I agree, looking over your left shoulder, as if something happening behind you has caught my attention. But it's just so I don't have to meet your gaze. You have a way of seeing right through me to the core. I couldn't even lie to you when the lie was for something sweet, like pretending I'd forgotten our anniversary so I could surprise you with a fancy dinner.

"I've been ... in the wilderness too," I say. "On another planet, if you want to know the truth."

I let that sit. I'm hoping it will be enough of a distraction. But you're quiet for only a few moments, taking it in.

Then, "How did you get there?" I can see the hope written on your face. "With ... my Pure Dark Energy?"

I shake my head no. I can see you're disappointed. "Ang—" I catch myself before calling you *Angie*. That's another life, not this one. Here I was expecting to call you Dr. Corliss for a while longer. "—gela," I continue,

"I feel like it's going to take me hours to tell you the whole thing." *Hours and too many lies.* "But the short version: I met some extraterrestrials about ten years back. They brought some of their tech and taught me how to use it. Even ... how to make it. But then they left, and it's taken me this long to find them on their own planet."

"But you did," you say, your voice quiet and low, the way it gets when you're excited but careful not to show it. The way you had to learn to be around your fellow scientists.

It makes me sad to see you do it to me. We shared everything. Neither of us ever held back.

"I did," I agree. "And they taught me even more—a lot more. Including how to skip back a year—" *Lie.* More than a year. "—and bring you in on this. If—that is, if you're willing to work with me."

And there's that smile again. It splits my heart in two. But it also lights me up like a bonfire. It's taking me everything I have not to reach out for you, fold you into my arms, hold you like I've been aching to do all this time we've been apart.

You stick out your hand. I was right, it's cold as I shake it.

"Reggie Swan," you say, "I'm happy to join the team. But now you're going to have to tell me absolutely everything."

Absolutely everything. Not even close. But I can tell you what you told me to say, and that will have to do.

First I stall some more. I'm not ready to rush into it.

"Do you want me to show you how these work?"

It's irresistible. I knew it would be. You allow me to distract you a little longer.

"What do you notice?" I ask, indicating the pod's soft rose-gold interior.

It only takes you a few seconds. "No controls?"

I shake my head and point at my temple. You smile. I knew you'd like it.

"Telepathy?"

"Yes," I say. "Good enough description."

"How? Can I think to it right now?"

"We have to pair you with one first," I say. "It needs to feel you inside it. Want to try one?"

You laugh. "Do you need to ask?"

"I'll open it," I say, showing off a little. I'm paired with all of the pods at the Factory, so any of them will respond to my thoughts.

Mentally, I ask the nearest one to open its lid. Not a command, but a request. *Please open. Thank you.*

More of my courtly manners, I suppose, but some of the pilots had to learn the hard way that these craft can think for themselves. And they do not like being disrespected.

The lid smoothly glides open and tucks itself into the

lower half. You reach out and touch the open rim. Always wanting to experience things for yourself.

I offer my hand to help you in. You take it.

Goddamn, woman, can't you feel it?

The way our fingers find each other so naturally. The energy that passes between our skin. The heat. The vibrancy. The *familiarity*.

I'm like a school boy having to hold back a racing heart and my panting breath. I hold onto your hand as long as seems decent, but then I let go before I say something I shouldn't.

You act like nothing's happened on your end. And maybe it's no act. Why should you feel a single thing for me? You only just met me yesterday, and that was while you could barely keep awake. If my little markers, showing up in your life here and there, have done anything to make you remember me, you sure don't seem affected.

I feel an unexpected deflation. What did I expect? Something. Not nothing.

You settle yourself into the seat of the pod.

I'm back to being your host.

"Rest your arms there," I say, pointing to the two projections at either side of the seat. "Let your hands extend over the edge of the arm rests. Try to let it get as much contact as it can with you ... that's right."

You shift a little, getting more comfortable. The arm

rests fold around your arms, gently cupping them from elbows to wrists. You give a little gasp of surprise. But then you smile. I know you. Of course you're delighted. A new toy. One that works in unexpected ways.

"Now your feet," I say. Before I can suggest it, you kick off your shoes. You don't go the extra step of removing your socks, but this is good enough. You rest your feet against the angled panel at the base of the pod.

"It's reading you," I tell you. "Just a little bit longer."

"This is the most comfortable chair I've ever sat in," you say.

"It would be. It always is for whoever's sitting there."

I give it a few minutes. Longer than it actually takes. But I want to give myself that same time. I need to keep a clear head. You don't know me. I have to remember myself.

"That should probably do it," I say.

"So what's next?"

"I find they like to be complimented."

You chuckle at that and look at me to make sure I'm not joking. I'm not.

"That's easy," you say. "Lots to admire."

You close your eyes for a bit. There's a soft smile resting on your lips.

Then you open your eyes again. "It's a she," you tell me.

"That she is," I say. "We have all kinds. Now see if she'll close her lid for you."

Your smile leaves. You're concentrating. It doesn't take a lot of effort. Just a simple straight-forward thought, and the lid of your pod glides up and over your head.

A second later, it glides back open. You must have asked it to.

"We used to use head gear," I say. "Fancy headbands to connect us to the pods. We thought we had to, to communicate with them. Turns out we were making it much harder than we had to."

"Don't I know that experience," you say. You hold your arm out to me, a signal you'd like help climbing back out of the pod. I clasp your hand again. My palm is sweaty. I'm sure you must be able to feel it. Damn school boy. If you knew me, we could laugh about it right now.

But if you notice, you're not letting on. Instead, you're right back to your original question. Dog with a bone, not giving it up.

As soon as I help you back on your feet and you're standing beside me: "The time loop," you say. "Tell me. We can get back to the pods later."

I suppress a sigh. In your place, I'd be the same. I'd want to know. No more fiddling around.

"Time loop is ten years," I say.

You watch my face, clearly expecting more. When I don't offer it, you narrow your eyes just a bit. Impatient.

"Kirsten said something about ten years ago *and* ten years from now."

I need to talk to that woman about not giving away all my punchlines.

"That's right," I tell you. "Twenty years so far, backward and forward."

"I don't pretend to know how that works," you say. "I understand it, theoretically, but I've never been in a situation where someone can tell me it's real."

You look at me again, maybe willing me to say it still is a theory, we're not really sure, we *think* it might work this way...

But that would be a lie. "It's real," I say. "As real as you standing here."

Your eyes widen. But not out of fear or nervousness. I can see that. I know you're excited. Ready to learn something new, something big.

If you only knew the full truth. But I can't tell you all of it. You made me swear. I would never break my promise to you.

Even though I've been regretting it for the past several hours.

"Buy you a coffee?" I ask. Stalling. Still stalling.

But the offer lights you up. I know your head is probably pounding right now. Your caffeine addiction is real. Or at least was, in our other life. I wonder now if it still is.

If maybe the many things I think I know about your aren't necessarily true this time.

I'm not sure I like that idea. But at the same time, it's also intriguing. Who are you now, Angela Corliss? What surprises do you have for me in this loop?

"Coffee." You close your eyes briefly, as if I've just said the magical word. Then you look at me and smile. "Someplace private. I don't want to be interrupted. Because you, Mr. Swan, are about to *talk*."

4

Science is a story to me. I could hear about science all day every day. Sit at someone's feet while they explain what they've wondered, what they tried, what they discovered.

This man Reggie Swan.

The stories he knows.

We sat in some kind of break room for what might have been three or four hours, me drinking coffee and munching on nuts and an apple and some chocolate they had on hand, interrupting him only when I needed more details, more explanation, but then letting him talk and talk and tell me.

Dear God, the things that man knows.

The things that man has done.

And even though I already saw it last night, my eyes kept going back to his left hand, that platinum ring on his wedding finger, as if this were a date we were on, not a lengthy interview between fellow scientists.

Although he wanted me to understand he is not a scientist. "Just a maker."

Just a maker. Spare me. A man who could invent what he has invented and has made the kind of advanced discoveries Reggie Swan has—that is citizen science at its core. He didn't need a physics degree like mine to do all he's done. That man's mind is superior to anyone's I've ever met.

As we rolled into hour four I could feel the day's strain. So much to learn and absorb. And just trying to get by on coffee and snacks.

"They make a reasonable dinner here," Reggie said. "Maybe we should take a break."

I smiled at that. But I was serious when I told him, "You're going to have to be the one to regulate this. Because I can honestly keep going all night. Right now I am an open vessel. I want everything you can possibly pour into it."

And then he did something I didn't expect. He started to reach for my hand, his fingers were almost to mine, when he abruptly pulled them back as if I'd scalded him. Fingers touching flame.

He got up from the plastic-topped table where we'd been sitting across from each other on standard-issue folding metal chairs. Same as in any university, any lab. Not meant for people to sink into and relax for too long, when there was important work to be done elsewhere.

I'll admit I was feeling pretty stiff by hour four, and I'd taken only one restroom break when I couldn't hold my coffee anymore, but other than that, what I said was true. I was in it for the long haul. I could sit there all night.

Then, I'm embarrassed to say, I did my awkward best to find out. That almost-touching of my hand felt like a reason.

"You must ... I mean, your wife must be waiting for you."

So blatant, so humiliatingly obvious. But it gave me the knowledge I needed.

Reggie smiled a sad smile. "She died, I'm very sorry to say."

"Oh." *Oh.* "I'm so sorry." And I was. And I wasn't.

"She was wonderful," Reggie said. "I miss her every day."

He seemed about to say more, but then he stopped himself.

"But we have our work, right?" he said. I nodded. I knew what he meant. A life of the mind is all-consuming. Except in those moments when it isn't.

I wasn't sure if I should ask, or if I actually wanted to know. But sometimes the mouth just moves on its own. "How long ago?"

"Ten years," Reggie said. He must have been in his early to mid-sixties then, close to my own age. He twisted the ring on his finger back and forth, what looked like absent-mindedly. But then he seemed to make up his mind about something.

He had to fight his finger a little to do it, but he got the ring free of it.

He pulled it off and tilted it to show me the engraving inside. Small, barely visible after however many years of wearing the ring against his skin, but I could see it once he pointed to it.

An A, underlined. <u>A</u>

"It was a joke," Reggie told me. "She put the ring on my finger and then told me about it later that night. It's the Bar A, like a brand." Reggie made a sizzling sound, like a brand against flesh. "I was hers, she was mine. I liked the idea so much, we took her ring back to the shop and had a Bar R engraved on that one." Reggie shrugged. He seemed embarrassed to share with a relative stranger something so intimate.

"What was her name?" I wasn't sure I wanted to keep talking about her, but the words just automatically kept coming.

Reggie stared at the ring. "Anne." He slipped the ring

back on his wedding finger. Then he stood up. "We need to eat. Come on."

And this time when he held out his hand he didn't take it away. I let him guide me to my feet.

If I held on a split-second longer than I should have...

So be it.

5

———

"There you are." Kirsten Simmens finds us in the cafeteria dining on stuffed manicotti and grilled zucchini. She sits beside Angela. "How are you feeling?"

Angela holds up her empty fork. "Better." She points the tines at me. "I wish I could go back thirty years. I feel like my whole career could have been different."

I look down at my plate. I can't bear to meet her eyes. To say something so innocent when it is the crux of my whole life.

I wish I had met her, too. Married her. Had twenty more years with her than I did.

That we haven't been separated these past ten. Do I get to count those as married years? I was married to her in my heart, even if she never knew it. Or knew me.

I stand up and pick up my plate. I need a temporary

escape. I can feel the heat on my face. I need to cool it down. Re-establish equilibrium.

"Need more?" I ask.

Angela shakes her head and spears another chunk of manicotti. I turn to Kirsten. "Anything?"

Kirsten looks at me strangely.

For a moment I can't unlock my gaze. It is as if she is holding me there.

Some electrical or gravitational force. Something out of my control.

I have known Kirsten Simmens for nearly thirty years now. Part of it is in a life she doesn't know. And she never knew me in my married years. That was a whole other lifetime.

But there is a resonance between our minds. A certain frequency she taught me about when we both lived on base with our extraterrestrial friends RayJay, Linus, and Mit.

It's been a long time since I have felt her mind locked onto mine.

"Second life?"

The fear of it snaps me free. How did she hear me when I tried so hard not to think it? Everything has to go as planned. We worked it out, you and me. I can't risk a single wrong move.

"Let it go," I warn Kirsten in my mind, and I walk away with my plate.

She doesn't follow me physically. She doesn't need to.

"Reggie—"

I quit walking. But I can't face her. *"Please."*

Then I can feel the memories flooding through my brain, and there is nothing I can do to stop them. The way RayJay taught me to search the universe for the one my heart longed for. The moment I found Angela Corliss. The way I *knew*. Absolutely knew.

The same way RayJay taught me to navigate the universe. Locking on to my destination and instantly finding myself there. The thrilling and unexpected ease of it.

Angela was my destination. But there was no guarantee our life together would go on and on. Humans are fragile. Humans die. No matter how much they are loved.

But you are wise, sweetheart. Brilliant. Your mind operates at a level no one else's can.

And time is mutable. RayJay taught me that. Past, present, future, all of it happening at the same time in different slices, so that what you think hasn't happened yet already has, just on a different slice of your timeline.

You died. I watched you. It broke my heart to watch you.

But—and—we already had this other plan. You looped out of your old life into this second one. You never really died. No matter what my eyes thought I saw.

"Please," I beg Kirsten. *"She can't know. She doesn't want to know."*

I turn back and look at both of them. At you calmly polishing off your dinner, at Kirsten calmly gazing back at me.

To my relief, Kirsten just smiles.

She doesn't seem surprised by any of it.

"I've seen a lot of unbelievable things," she reminds me.

I watch her say something to Angela, then Kirsten gets up and comes walking toward me.

I can feel my heart panicking. I might have just ruined my chances. Things aren't unfolding the way they should be. We had everything so carefully planned out.

Not that I stuck to it all, letter for letter. Those times when I couldn't resist coming to see you, even for just a brief glance, a momentary interaction. I admit it, I haven't been pure about our plan. But it's a lot to ask of a man to stay away from the one he loves. I did my best. But knowing you were alive in my world was just too impossible to ignore. Maybe someone else could have kept to our strict no-contact rules, knowing the consequences if it didn't work. But over time, all the years without you, it turned out I couldn't do it.

And now I'm a stranger to you and you have no reason to trust me. You could leave here tomorrow and go on with your second life, and I would have to let you go. I can't interfere. You have to live it the way you are meant to live it. We both agreed on that.

And if we met again—when we met again—we would fall in love or we wouldn't. Although you were so sure you would. You told me so. Like a puzzle piece slipping into place.

Kirsten stands beside me now and speaks quietly out loud, rather than in my mind.

"You should tell her. She can take it. You have no idea what we just went through. She's strong and she's brave. Trust me, she'll want to know."

Kirsten lays a hand briefly on my shoulder, then walks on.

But not without a parting thought, mind to mind.

"Come on, Reggie, haven't you both lost enough time already?"

6

In my past you say you knew me. I don't remember. I've tried to. I try to picture it the way you've described it. But it's not there. That past is a blank.

But this present is here. This future is creating itself second by second, right in front of us.

You have a ring that fits me perfectly, even though my left ring finger is not a typical size. I fell off my bike when I was young and the bone never properly healed. But when you showed it to me—engraved with the **R**, the Bar R—and I slid it over the misaligned second joint, the ring settled perfectly into place as if it had always been there. I'm never taking it off.

It's just like you. Familiar, comfortable, right. The kind of man I would have wanted to be with in this life or any other. Loving, wise, and unbelievably smart. Resourceful and safe. The kind of man a lost and hungry kitten would come running to. The kind that extraterrestrials know they can trust their secrets to and can teach how to take the human race further.

The kind a physicist on the run who has to completely remake her life again would choose to be by her side. I choose you. Let's go forward and make something new.

My life is not what I expected it to be. Yours isn't, either. And here we are.

This age, this place, these experiences, this time.

Second life, third life, maybe more lives than I can count—it doesn't matter. I know what I know. It's here in the hearts of both of us. I believe we will find each other every time.

And for now, this particular present and this future, you are taking me to meet your friends and find out everything I want to know. And since I want to know everything, we might be gone a long time.

Although what is time once you learn to move backward and forward, just as distance means nothing once you understand the true secret to travel.

We leave tomorrow on a second honeymoon, this time out to the stars where you found your friends RayJay, Mit, and Linus, and where you learned from them how to find me the first time, and then how to find me again.

The heart has its own map, you told me. It knows exactly where to go.

Across galaxies, across time, across lives.
From now on I'm coming with you.

YOU WILL FIND MORE stories about Reggie Swan and Angela Corliss in the book MAKER, part of the Dove Season Universe by Robin Brande.

RURAL ROUTE

INTRODUCTION

While walking down a dusty country road as a child, Jenna finds a secret letter delivered to her from out of the past.

It is the beginning of a miraculous correspondence that will shape the rest of Jenna's future.

A tale of nostalgia and a magic that spans the generations.

1

Whenever Jenna baked she thought of Grandma Ada.

Not because they were her recipes, most of them weren't.

But because Jenna used butter that came in sticks. Flour she bought at the store. Eggs that came six to a carton, cleaned up, not coated in chicken waste.

And mostly because Jenna mixed with an electric mixer, a luxury Grandma Ada wouldn't have dreamed of back in 1926.

Jenna didn't have to guess at that. She had it in her grandmother's own words.

I saw you today. Did you see me? Write me back. Love, Ada.

A note Jenna found in the back pocket of her off-brand jeans back when she was eight years old.

She was bored on the trip. She wanted to go back to Arvada, a little suburb just outside Denver, where the grown version of Grandma Ada lived in a nice clean house on a street where there were tons of kids to play with.

Her fun grandma who liked to put on Patti Page records and dance around the living room while Jenna and her little sister Margie giggled.

And Granddad Earl was down in the basement watching news or sports, but he never seemed bothered when Jenna and Margie came to bother him.

He'd turn off the TV and ask them, "What's doin', girls?" and they'd go into great detail about how they spent their day.

Then if it was before dinner Granddad Earl would sneak the girls upstairs and dish them out ice cream even though it was sure to spoil their appetites.

Grandma Ada would come in and scold him, "Oh, Earl!" but she let Jenna and Margie finish their scoops of vanilla even though she already had something wonderful cooking in the oven.

Every summer Jenna looked forward to her two weeks at her favorite grandparents'. But the summer she was eight, Jenna's mother wanted to take a separate day trip to bring them someplace special.

"It's where Grandma Ada grew up," she said. "Out on the prairie. Don't you want to see that?"

"Is Grandma coming?" Jenna asked.

"No, she said she spent enough time there," Jenna's mother said. "But I want to see it."

So they drove about an hour from Arvada to the small college town of Greeley, and then a half hour further still. Out to a town that didn't exist anymore. Purcell, Colorado. Now nothing but flat, dry grassland for miles around, without any houses or even a single tree.

They drove on paved county roads for a few miles, then dirt roads from then on. And all the while Jenna kept waiting for something worth seeing. So far the only thing had been some cows and horses behind shabby-looking farm fences they passed along the way.

And the smell. Like manure, but worse. Like stockyards and dirty animals. It seemed like a horrible place to live.

It was hard to believe her clean grandma once lived out here.

Finally Jenna's father turned left onto a narrow dirt road and parked the Buick over at the side.

"This is it!" Jenna's mother announced.

They all got out of the car. Jenna's mother was smiling, taking pictures. Jenna's father stood with his hands on his hips and looked around pretending to be impressed.

Jenna and her six-year-old sister Margie rolled their

eyes at each other. Jenna wished she had brought along a book to read.

"Can you imagine?" Jenna's mother said. "Your grandma's father was a homesteader out here. He built everything from scratch. His house, his barn, the windmill..."

Jenna looked around. She couldn't see any of that.

"Then they lost it all after too many years of terrible drought," Jenna's mother said. "Your grandma told me that one day the bank sent trucks to her house and they took away all the animals."

"What animals?" Jenna asked, perking up. Finally, something that sounded interesting. She had a black and white cat named Toby. She couldn't imagine some bank sending people to take him away.

"The horses and cows," her mother said. "It was a terrible day. After that your grandma's family had nothing left anymore. They had to leave here and move back to Arvada."

That sounded fine to Jenna. Why wouldn't they want to live in Arvada anyway?

"Then ... well, your great-grandfather couldn't really cope anymore," Jenna's mother said. "He ... well, he shot himself not long after."

"Shot himself?" Margie repeated. She, too, had started listening once her mother mentioned the animals.

Jenna's mother rested her hands on Margie's shoulders. "It was a sad time. Your Grandma Ada doesn't really like to talk about it."

After about an hour of just walking along the dirt road under the blazing sun and looking at pale green grass as high as Jenna's knees, Margie finally started to whine. For once Jenna appreciated her for that.

"It's hot," Margie said. "I want to go back to Grandma's."

Jenna's mother sighed. "All right. I suppose we've seen as much as there is."

It was while Jenna was walking back to the Buick that she felt a slight tug on the back pocket of her Walmart jeans. Like someone had caught the pocket briefly with her fingers.

Jenna scratched at the area. And heard the wrinkling of a piece of paper.

The rest of her family was a little ahead, so no one was watching as she reached into her pocket and pulled the paper out.

It looked like a piece of newspaper or a page torn out of an old magazine. She could see the bottom parts of a few advertisements, one for a new tractor, another for a strange-looking kind of rake.

But the bottom few inches of the page had an empty space. And someone had written there in pencil with what looked like careful but childish handwriting.

I saw you. Did you see me? Write me back. Love, Ada.

Jenna turned in a circle on the road, looking around her in every direction.

There was no one there.

Hot dust blew in her face. And with it, a kind of thrill went through her.

Something very mysterious was going on.

She shouldn't be surprised. It was June twenty-first, the Summer Solstice, and in the book she left at her grandparents' a group of kids were out in the woods on Summer Solstice when they found a space alien hiding in the bushes.

There was a portal the alien came through that was only open that one day a year.

Maybe Jenna had stumbled on a portal of her own, out here in the dry, dusty prairie with no one for miles around.

And if it was only open today, just this one day, she had to do something quickly before it went away.

Jenna ran to catch up with her mother. "Can I have a piece of paper?"

"Sure, honey." Her mother rummaged through her purse where Jenna knew she kept a little spiral notebook to make all her endless lists. "Why?"

"I want to write something down before I forget."

It wasn't unusual. Jenna was always writing down

poems and songs and stories. She had what her parents called an active imagination. Jenna always took that as a matter of pride.

She borrowed her mother's ball-point pen and quickly scribbled a note in answer.

Hi. My name is Jenna. I am 8 years old. How old are you? Where are you? Are you real? Write me back.

Jenna ran back to where she felt the tug on her pocket. She looked around for a safe place to leave her note.

There was a large round stone about the size of a toaster off at the side of the road. She slipped the note under the rock and waited.

And waited.

The sun beat down on her, but she didn't care anymore. She held her breath, hoping.

Her father honked the horn.

"Just a minute!" Jenna shouted.

Another minute passed, and he honked again.

"I have to leave," Jenna said to whoever might be listening. "I live in Phoenix, Arizona, but I'm staying with my grandparents in Arvada. Maybe you can find me there."

She turned reluctantly back toward the Buick.

And felt another tug on the back pocket of her jeans.

She whipped around, but no one was there.

Jenna smiled. She wasn't afraid.

She pulled out a second note from her pocket.

I am 8. I have 2 sisters and a little brother. My daddy made this farm. My mama used to live in Arvada. Write me back. Ada Ralston, Rural Route 11.

Jenna knew the name Ralston. It was her grandmother's maiden name.

She almost whispered that to her new invisible friend.

But Jenna's father honked the horn a third time and Jenna decided to keep that secret to herself. For now.

She waved to the air. "Bye! I'll write!"

She ran back to the car and dove into the back seat next to Margie.

"What was all that about?" her mother asked.

"I like it here," Jenna said. "Can we come back tomorrow?"

She wasn't sure the portal would stay open beyond Summer Solstice, but she'd still try.

Jenna's mother smiled with surprise. "You really want to?"

"No," Margie blurted out. "I hate it here. It's hot and smelly and boring."

Jenna's father chuckled. "Afraid I have to agree."

"Just you and me, then," Jenna said to her mother. "Please?"

After just a moment's hesitation, Jenna's mother nodded. "All right, just you and me."

Back at her grandparents' house that night, Jenna wrote a five-page letter in the neatest handwriting she could. Filled with details about herself and her life.

She felt tempted to show it to her grandmother.

But what if this was something magical? What if her grandmother might die or go into shock if Jenna told her she might have met her ghost or whatever it was back on the road in Purcell?

What if it wasn't her grandmother at all, but some other girl with the same name?

Jenna never considered that she that might have made the whole thing up. She might have an active imagination, but she wasn't crazy.

She folded the five-page letter and put it in a pale blue envelope she found in her grandmother's desk.

Then the next day Jenna and her mother drove back out to Purcell, where Jenna secretly hid the letter under the special rock at the side of the road.

She walked back and forth up that section of tall grass, giving Ada Ralston time to write her back.

Jenna's mother took more photographs. She seemed happy just to quietly stare out over the grassland toward the ridge of mountains far off in the distance.

"Can you imagine?" she said at one point. "Don't you think it would have been so lonely out here?"

So lonely you'd be desperate for a friend. For any little girl you saw walking along the road.

When the hour was over and there had been no tug on Jenna's pocket, she thought to look under the rock.

There were three scraps of paper there, with writing in every available space.

"I have to go," Jenna whispered to Ada. "But I'll be back again, I promise."

Although she wasn't sure when. Their two-week visit to Arvada was almost over. She doubted she could convince her mother to come out again tomorrow, when it was their last day.

Jenna carefully folded the scraps of paper and stowed them in her pocket where she could read them later.

It was the beginning of ten years of secret correspondence.

2

As soon as the brownies cooled, Jenna wrapped them in foil and set them on the passenger seat of her forest green Subaru Outback. It was Saturday, the day she always made the drive from her modest three-bedroom ranch home in Greeley to visit her grandmother in Arvada.

Jenna was forty-seven now. Grandma Ada was ninety-five.

Arvada might as well be considered Denver now. Her grandparents' house had been demolished years ago to make way for more freeway. Now chain stores and restaurants and new upscale neighborhoods filled in whatever gaps there had once been between the surrounding suburbs and the larger city.

One of the new buildings at the edge of Arvada was

the assisted living facility where Grandma Ada had been living for the past two years.

Up on the third floor, the "Memory Care" unit. A nice name for the dementia ward.

Jenna and Grandma Ada were the only ones in the family who lived in Colorado. Jenna's parents had retired to Glendale, Arizona, and Margie worked at a tech company in San Francisco. Jenna's mother came to visit Grandma Ada a few times a year. The weekly visits fell to Jenna.

They were visits she was happy to make.

She had moved to Greeley after high school, to be as close as she could to Purcell.

She told her parents it was because she had always wanted to go to Northern Colorado University, *Go Bears!*

She got her degrees in English Literature and History.

Even though there was really only one history she cared about.

The letters had come to an abrupt and depressing end when Jenna was eighteen.

Ada Ralston was eighteen then, too. It was 1936 in her time. Jenna knew the end was coming, but she thought it was only the end to the farm, not Ada's letters.

Jenna knew from her mother's stories that the day would come when the bank would send out trucks to haul off all the Ralstons' horses and cows.

Jenna didn't know the exact date. But when she

eagerly retrieved Ada's letters from under the rock during that year's Summer Solstice, the worst hadn't happened yet. The letters—one written in each month, and saved for the Solstice's special delivery—described Ada's father's desperate attempts to still save the farm after years of endless drought.

Jenna considered writing back what she knew. To give Ada at least some warning of what was to come at some point later that year.

But in the end Jenna decided that knowing the worst wouldn't help Ada feel any better now.

Especially since Jenna also knew that Ada's father would shoot himself once he lost the farm.

The last five years had already been filled with too much tragedy. Ada lost her favorite sister to scarlet fever. Ada's mother died a year later of pneumonia, alone in a hospital in Greeley that was too far away for the children to visit. The family still didn't have a car. It would have meant a long journey by horse and cart, and Ada's father couldn't spare the horse.

As the oldest, Ada now took care of her remaining sister and their little brother. She took over all the cooking and cleaning, too. She had to quit school to do it.

Her father drank too much. He sometimes hit Ada and the younger kids. It was all written out in Ada's lovely penmanship on whatever paper she could scrounge from around the farm.

But now you're coming back to visit, Ada wrote in her last letter. *How I wish I could talk to you face to face!*

Jenna had still never told her Grandma Ada about the letters. Or told Ada Ralston that she would grow up to be Jenna's grandmother.

She kept the two worlds separate. To do otherwise felt like interfering with what might turn out to be delicate magic.

When Jenna returned to Purcell the following year, there were no letters beneath the rock.

Nor the next year, nor any year after that, even though Jenna checked every single Summer Solstice.

The correspondence was over.

Jenna carefully stored away every letter.

"Look, Ada," the care worker Denise said, "it's your granddaughter, the writer!"

They all referred to Jenna that way. It seemed to help Grandma Ada place her.

The little library downstairs on the first floor of the assisted living facility was filled with historical romances by Jenna Ralston. Mainly stories that took place before and during the Dust Bowl. It was Jenna's specialty as a history professor at Northern Colorado University in Greeley.

Grandma Ada's room had its own collection of the books, all signed warmly by the author herself. *To my best grandma, Ada. Thank you for sharing your life with me. Love, Jenna.*

Jenna always resisted adding, *Write me back.*

Every Saturday she brought another stack of Ada's letters to read out loud to her.

Grandma Ada would smile and nod. Or sometimes cry if the news was awful.

Jenna was never sure if Grandma Ada realized she wrote the letters herself.

"Her mother *died*?" Grandma Ada said when Jenna read her that particular letter. Tears gathered in the old woman's pale blue eyes. "That's so sad! She never got to see her again." Then she sighed. "They all lived such a hard life."

But then a short while later as Jenna read the next letter from that same year, Grandma Ada said, "You know, my mother was very beautiful. But she was a city girl. She could never survive on the farm."

Grandma Ada seemed to especially love all the details of every day life on the farm. The names of the horses. The meals her mother used to cook. How her father shot jackrabbits for supper every Sunday.

"We didn't have toilet paper," Grandma Ada interjected one day.

"What did you do?" Jenna asked, even though she already knew the answer from other letters.

"We kept a stack of old newspapers and corn cobs out in the outhouse," Grandma Ada said. She squirmed in her faded pink recliner as if reliving the discomfort.

Jenna loved all the details, too. Because reading them

back when she was a girl had profoundly changed her life.

From the time she was eight, she never, ever took her comforts for granted. The family's car. Soft toilet paper. Her nice clean clothes. Being able to take a bath whenever she wanted. Hot water that came right out of the faucet.

Being able to go to school every day and not have to quit to take care of her little sister.

Jenna sometimes played make-believe, pretending to be a girl out on the prairie. Margie hated that game. She didn't want to have to wash out her clothes by hand or sweep the whole house when they had a vacuum.

Margie loved technology of any kind.

Jenna sometimes regretted how far the modern world had come.

It was why she still knitted and crocheted. Still baked from scratch. Why she sewed her own clothes and then wore them until they fell apart.

Why she still wrote letters by hand and saved all the ones her grandmother wrote her back.

"Do you remember?" she asked Grandma Ada one day as she sat beside her holding her soft, withered hand. "I was your friend Jenna. You wrote to me. All these letters are from you."

Grandma Ada smiled at her, that cheerful but vacant smile that made Jenna wonder if anyone was home.

"You dressed like a boy," Grandma Ada said. "I saw you. You wore pants and I wore a dress."

"Yes!" Jenna said, squeezing her hand. "Yes, Grandma, that was me."

But then the brief light in Grandma Ada's eyes faded again. She was tired. The visit had worn her out.

Jenna got up and kissed her grandmother's forehead. She smoothed her hand down Ada's soft cheek.

Ada raised her own shaky hand and held Jenna's there.

She tilted her head back and gazed into Jenna's eyes.

"You were my best friend," she whispered.

"You were mine, too," Jenna said, the words choking in her throat. "For the longest time. But why did you stop writing to me?"

"We went away," Grandma Ada said. "We lost the farm. I couldn't find you anymore."

Jenna thought of all the times she had walked up and down the dirt road of old Purcell, searching under rocks, hoping for more.

How she had moved to Greeley once the letters stopped, to make sure she'd be nearby if they ever came again.

How she spent hours on that road every Summer Solstice, convinced that the magic could still happen if she still believed.

But maybe this was magic enough. To still have the

letters written on old newspaper and torn pages from old magazines, written either thirty-nine or eighty-seven years ago, depending on which world the two correspondents lived in.

"Better go now," Grandma Ada said, her voice sounding feeble and tired. "It's almost supper." She brought Jenna's palm to her lips and kissed it the way she used to when Jenna was a child.

"Think I'll have ice cream before supper," Jenna said. She flashed her grandmother a mischievous smile.

"You do that," Grandma Ada said, chuckling. "You're a good girl. My Jenna gets to do whatever she wants."

Jenna thought about that as she rode the elevator down to the first floor.

How her life must have looked to her grandmother when she was a child.

How much freedom it must have seemed that she had, this girl from the future with the strange clothes and the futuristic car.

My Jenna gets to do whatever she wants.

Jenna couldn't disagree.

It was the privilege of modern life. To get to drive her car, eat takeout, watch a movie at home any time she wanted while she crocheted herself a sweater or baked bread from scratch.

She still straddled both worlds, living between the old and the new. None of her friends really understood.

"You're allowed to use a blow dryer," her friend Carol told her when Jenna showed up to teach at the university one January morning, shivering because her long graying hair was still wet.

Everyone always thought she took it too far. But it was Jenna's way of honoring Grandma Ada, who never had a different choice. Every day out on the prairie was hard.

Jenna didn't romanticize it in her books. She showed the homesteaders' lives the way they were.

And her readers loved every detail, just like Jenna had as a child.

To watch a real life unfold, in all its hardship and its grit.

To know that young Ada Ralston would one day grow up to move to the city and live in a lovely home. That she would marry a nice man named Earl and have a daughter and two granddaughters.

That Ada would see those girls one day, and find a way to slip one a letter.

Through a magic Jenna still didn't understand, but was grateful for every day.

She started up her Outback and turned on the air conditioning.

She looked up at the third floor windows, the way she always did.

Grandma Ada was sitting where she could look out

the window. Jenna reached her hand out the window of her car and waved until Grandma Ada waved back.

I saw you. Did you see me?

Jenna returned her precious letters to the covered basket she had learned to weave herself, and that she had lined with fine pink satin.

Then Jenna drove back to the privileged future her grandmother had made possible for her only by being tough enough to survive.

THE BRIDGE

INTRODUCTION

What if death isn't the end?

Laney's husband died in an avalanche nine days ago. But that can't be the end. Not yet.

She has one last hope to contact him. But the price may be more than she realizes.

A tale of love, loss, and a hope for a new beginning.

1

People still did normal things.

Couples who spent their Sunday morning in bed sat at outside tables on the restaurant patio now holding hands and sharing secret smiles.

It wasn't winter here. Just a six-hour flight away, from the mountains of Canada to the desert of southern Arizona, and it was spring already and hot.

The open walls of the patio were wrapped in dark green mesh shade cloth that let in the fresh air but cut the sun. Misters were set in the ceiling every few feet, raining down refreshing droplets. The patio was dark and cool. I needed that. I'd only just come back from snow.

If Danny and I had started for home just a few days earlier, the first week of April instead of the second, he would still be alive.

I knew I shouldn't keep thinking that way, but I couldn't stop it.

The hostess sat me at one of the three small tables on the raised platform at the very back of the patio. From here I could see all the brunchers down below, people in shorts and tank tops, a few obviously coming from church with their dressier clothing, but the women still with bare arms and bare legs, some of the men in nice slacks and flip flops.

Everyone understood the Tucson dress code. Already we were all wearing as little as possible. It was supposed to be ninety-seven degrees by the afternoon.

I saw Louise from the distance. She always stood out, but now even more than usual. She was thinner—much thinner—than I remembered, and wore a pale green fleece ski cap over her short white-blonde hair. Everything else was to code: shorts, short-sleeved T-shirt, hiking sandals. It was just the warm winter hat that was wrong.

Louise's almost transparently-blue eyes scanned the tables, looking for me. I could see people staring at her, the way I did the first time I saw her in one of our college psych lectures, most of them probably trying to decide the same way I did whether those pale eyes and her darkly tanned skin and naturally platinum hair made her look attractive or just spookily exotic.

Once I got to know her I realized she was beautiful from the inside out. But I could understand the looks people were giving her now, a mixture of surprise, curiosity, and suspicion. The way you might look at a witch and wonder if she was there to save you or to steal your soul.

I raised my arm. Louise saw me and gave me a big smile. But she didn't look well. And her walk confirmed it.

A halting kind of limp to her steps. A tight constriction of her arms, not swinging freely, athletically the way they always used to. She was a runner and swimmer, hiker, backpacker, outside every day one way or the other. She was only thirty-two, like me, but she looked decades older now.

I stood up as she mounted the two steps up onto the platform. I hugged her, but not as hard as I planned to. Her skeleton felt small and brittle inside my arms. But she still gave me a hard squeeze of her own, maybe trying to prove she wasn't as bad as she looked.

We sat down and she didn't make me wait.

"It's not cancer," she said. "I know it looks like it. It's a bunch of other things. Too boring to go into."

We were friends, even if we only saw each other every couple of years anymore. I was allowed to ask. "What's with the hat?"

She stuck her finger under the fleece and lifted it a few inches. She had hair under there, but not much of it.

"My head is always cold," she said. "Even a day like today."

"Whatever it is," I said, "I'm sorry."

Louise shrugged. "Danny. He's what I'm sorry about. It's awful, Laney. He was absolutely the best."

I nodded. I was exhausted from hearing about him. Exhausted from talking about him. I'd heard it all and said it all during every waking hour over the past nine days. I felt wrung dry. Fragile. Like a flimsy container whose walls were too thin to hold any more without bursting.

Louise looked into my eyes. She knew why she was there.

"Ready to order?" the cheerful server asked us.

"Just toast," Louise said. "And I'll stick with water."

I wasn't sick. Some part of me wanted to rebel against whatever it was making Louise look like that, lose her hair, have to wear a fleece cap, be down to that skeletal weight.

I ordered chocolate crêpes and an omelette. Even though my appetite was closer to Louise's. But you have to fight wherever you can fight.

That's what Danny always said.

I waited until we were alone again.

"Can you still do it?" I asked.

Louise coughed a few times and took a sip of water to calm it down. She nodded while she drank.

"I'm still afraid of it, you know," I said quietly.

"I know." Louise reached over and squeezed my hand.

"It's just this once. We'll do it for Danny." She unfolded her napkin and spread it across her lap. "We'll eat something first. Then you can follow me back to my house."

2

I'd only been to her current house once, and that was more than five years ago. Louise's white Mazda turned left before I was expecting it. I followed her through the run-down looking neighborhood to her red brick house at the end of a cul-de-sac.

Her white wooden door and the white trim around all the windows could have used a fresh paint job the last time I was here. Now everything looked cracked and chipped and flaking after baking that much longer in the sun.

Louise always had money, but she refused to spend it. One Christmas I bought her a new iron to replace the one she had inherited from her mother because the cord was so frayed it was clearly a fire hazard.

When I came over a few Christmases later I saw that

same old legacy iron sitting on the ironing board in her guest room.

"It still works," she told me when I gave her grief about it. "I'll use yours when this one craps out."

She had the same attitude toward her houses. This was the fourth one she'd lived in since I met her, and each house kept getting older, smaller, and shabbier.

"It's just me and the dogs," she told me. "They sleep on my bed. Why do we need so much room?"

She parked under the single-car carport. I parked my Jeep at the curb.

Maybe it was stupid, meeting at the restaurant first. I could have gotten the address from her again and come straight here.

But I still wasn't sure I was going to ask her, right up until the moment I did.

"Can you still do it?"

It was the only thing about Louise that I ever hated.

The only thing about her that truly scared me.

3

The house was surprisingly cold. All the shades
were drawn. The two dogs barked and wagged
from their side of the kiddie gate Louise had set across the
doorway of the kitchen.

"Bruce still chews," she said, setting them free. The
Great Pyrenees, Greta, trotted toward me in a dignified
way, but the younger one, Bruce, half-Lab half-insane,
came barreling toward me with his tongue lagging out the
side and paws already launching off the floor before I was
able to set my feet. His tongue was on my lips before I
could stop it.

"Down, Bruce, *down*," Louise scolded, but Bruce's love
was too real. He slurped my face with his overly wet
tongue and had no intention of letting me go.

Louise tugged him off by his flowery purple collar.

Bruce stared up at me with an adoring, loony look, wagging his tail so hard I could feel the air around us move.

Greta came forward then, her thick white coat making her look fifty pounds heavier than she probably was, and she looked me straight in the eyes the way some dogs do. She liked humans. She wanted to know what we thought.

I was afraid to kneel down to pet her with Bruce still trying to get back to my face, so I stroked my hand across her soft white head and returned her serious gaze.

"We'll go the guest room," Louise said. "Out," she told the dogs.

She opened the sliding glass door to her back patio, and here was someplace she had spent money. It was almost as nice as the restaurant patio, with similar looking shade cloth and two different misters at either end of the long stretch of concrete. Two plush-looking dog beds sat on the porch, along with numerous chew toys. I could see a few tennis balls in the grassy back yard beyond it.

I knew Louise was delaying things, for my sake, helping me ease into what we were about to do. I didn't try to rush her. I appreciated the time.

But at last the dogs were settled, and we were out of excuses. Louise looked at me, her pale blue eyes steady and questioning.

I sighed. "Okay."

The back bedroom had the same worn-down gray

carpeting as the rest of the house. The shades were drawn in here, too, and the room was pleasantly cool. There was a twin bed with a plain navy blue bedspread and single blue and white striped pillow, and a small computer desk with a folding metal chair. Louise's one concession to comfort was a second pillow draped over the seat.

An old-generation laptop sat closed on top of the desk. No need for the most current technology, with the kind of life Louise led.

Her communication with the world took a different form.

Louise crawled onto the bed and sat with her back propped against the wall, the pillow cushioning her spine. There was a blanket at the foot of the bedspread, and she draped it all around her, all the way up to her chin. All I could see was her face and the green fleece cap.

I turned the desk chair around and sat on top of its pillow and tried unsuccessfully to relax.

"It takes me longer now," Louise said.

"Okay." My pulse was already bounding ahead. I had watched her do this only once before, in college, and it scared me straight out of the room.

Louise closed her eyes. My eyes felt larger than normal, staring at her so hard.

I kept my breathing quiet.

Louise began to wheeze.

I knew things, things Louise had told me over the

years: Don't interfere. Don't try to stop her. What it felt like when someone did. How her heartbeat would become erratic. How her lungs wouldn't fill right, like someone had made her surface too quickly from a deep ocean dive.

It was a dive, in a way, she told me. So deep a human body shouldn't go there. Deeper and further than most human minds could stand.

But something she had been able to do since she was a child.

Then it began, the change that made me scream the first time I saw it, but I knew what to expect now, even though it was as terrifying as before.

It was her aura, she explained to me later, after the first time, when she found me sobbing on the landing outside her apartment. I had hurt her by running out of her bedroom the way I did—not hurt her feelings, hurt her heart and lungs and head. She didn't tell me that for several years. At the time she was more worried about consoling me.

I stared at it now, the gray blurring of her face, like someone had taken an eraser and smudged out her features. It enveloped her whole head, smearing out the color of her pale green cap, cloaking in gray all the human shapes of her face, her dark eyebrows, her eye sockets and nose and lips.

"I can teach you to see auras," she told me back then,

but I didn't want any part of it. It was witchcraft, voodoo, and it terrified me to my soul.

But she wasn't a witch. She could just see things. Hear things. Ask and know things.

"It's like some people have musical talent," she said. "This is just what I can do."

Her head seemed disembodied now, a gray puff of cloud hovering above the blanket. I hadn't stayed long enough to see anything more the first time. Everything from here on out was new.

There was a sound in the room, a faint buzzing, like an electrical hum I could feel thrumming in my own nerves. A cough rent through Louise's lungs, and the gray cloud cleared for a moment. I could see her face.

Her eyebrows were constricted. Her mouth looked tight and pursed, like she was in pain. But then the cough moved on and she was breathing steadily again, although I could still hear the wheeze.

Then her voice, not her voice.

"Laney."

I sat bolt upright on the chair.

The hairs on my arms rose as though the whole room were filled with static.

"Brainy Laney."

A sob erupted from my chest.

"I love you," Louise told me.

"I love you, too," I told Danny, my voice small and unsure.

"There was a bridge," he said.

"Yes."

"I fell through."

I nodded. "Yes."

It was a snow bridge, made of deceptive, windblown snow that hid the hundred-foot crevasse right beneath it. Danny was skiing with three other guys. They all made it across, Danny didn't.

Nobody knew it was there until Danny disappeared straight down.

It took them hours to bring his body out.

I had a massage that morning in town and then went to a movie by myself. I had no idea. I never felt it. No kind of sixth sense that something was wrong.

It was past nightfall before anyone called me. I'd baked a cherry lattice pie. I was going to reheat some pasta when he got home. I was worried, but I thought he probably stopped off for a few beers with the people he skied with. But someone from Search and Rescue called and he broke it to me slowly, too slowly, I already knew by the second sentence.

There was an incident this morning in the backcountry. Your husband...

All I could think was, *morning?* He's been dead all

along? What was I doing, going about my life, acting like everything was still the same? If I had known, I would have changed everything. I was ashamed by how stupid and frivolous I'd been.

That shame was still with me, even though I knew there was no point to it, but I couldn't make it go away. As if Danny could see me, as if it had hurt him, seeing me enjoying a massage, a movie, some pie.

He was dead. Didn't I care? Why wasn't I screaming from that moment on?

It was why I knew I could never cry enough. Never grieve enough. I had already lost my chance.

I sat on the soft leather couch in the vacation house we rented, feeling blank. Completely blank.

I didn't call anyone. It didn't seem necessary. None of this seemed real.

I fell asleep at some point in the night. When I woke I was still in a daze. Never? Never ever? I would never see my husband again?

I could see his body, the Search and Rescue guy said, but there was some damage—

I cut him off right there.

Hung up on him. He was probably used to it. People must react in various ways.

That phone call still hung over my head the next morning, like a chore I was putting off.

I should do the steps. Make arrangements.

But the whole day, I continued to sit. I must have had some water, used the bathroom, done something, but my whole world was as small as that one couch and the window across from it, looking out on the snow-covered mountains where my funny, handsome, adventurous and wonderful husband had skied only one day too many.

Just one day. If we had only left the week before, like we originally planned...

But the weather was too perfect. Blue skies, soft snow, an epic snow year. Why would we run away? We could make up the time at work later. We should enjoy our lives when they were right in front of us.

Even if we had left just the day before. Danny would still be alive.

Now it was Louise's turn to talk.

"Why were you here?" she asked Danny. "What was the purpose of your life?"

That was her gift, the questions. Listening for the answers. She didn't want to know the boring stuff, where did you hide the money, who killed you, did you feel pain. Other channelers could ask those questions, Louise told me. That wasn't why she was here.

She wanted the lessons from the soul. The larger picture that no one gets to know unless they can see it all laid out in front of them, like they were sitting on top of a platform with their feet dangling over the side, looking at the whole of their lifetime spread out below.

"To try things," Danny answered in the voice like Louise's, but not like Louise's regular voice at all. "To be fearless. To love Laney. To help her be happy."

The dam broke and I covered my face with my hands as tears flooded my eyes. I held back the sound of my sobs, I didn't want to wake Louise, but the force of trying to keep quiet felt like a stabbing pain inside my chest.

"Ask him—ask him—" I gulped back my sobs and tried to sound coherent. "Why did he have to go? Why so soon? Why did he only live thirty-three years?"

"I wanted to stay," he said.

"*Why didn't you?*" I cried.

Louise coughed then, a deep and rattling sound. The gray cloud of her aura striated across her face like horizontal lines on a faulty computer screen.

"No!" I said, reaching out a hand at her. Like I was losing Danny again.

Louise's breath wheezed harder than ever. Her forehead was creased with pain.

I knew I should get her water, help her somehow, but I couldn't, not yet.

I didn't want her to stop. It was selfish, but I needed her to keep going.

Louise gasped, deep and hard. The gray steadied across her face.

"Laney, I love you," she wheezed. "I've always loved you. I'll love you all your life."

"But you're gone," I told him, my voice crackling. "What was the point of all this?"

"To be alive," Danny said. "To love being alive. I wanted that and I got it."

Louise clutched at her chest through the blanket as another coughing fit overtook her. She bent forward, heaving.

Blood spattered the blanket.

I jumped from the chair and grabbed her. I held her as she gasped for air.

"Louise! You need help. I'm calling 911."

She waved her hand no, but more blood came out with the next cough. The session was over. The gray was gone. My friend was now struggling for her life.

I ran to the living room where I'd left my cell phone in my purse. I called 911. I had to run outside to look at the house number. "I have to get back to her!" I told the dispatcher. "Hurry!"

I could hear Louise's gasps as I ran back down the hall. I found her on the floor. Blood ran down her chin.

I lifted her head and tried to help her sit up. Her breathing seemed to get worse. Each gasp rattled louder. She squeezed my hand hard and looked into my eyes, and I could see the panic on her face.

"They're coming, Lou. They'll be here any minute."

And they were.

They rang the bell. I ran to let them in.

But we were too late.

Louise was gone.

4

I looked at her face before they covered it after they loaded her on a gurney.

I smoothed my thumb down her still-warm cheek.

I held her cooling fingers.

I kissed my friend on her forehead.

I had to give them all sorts of information. I only knew the answers to a fraction of their questions.

No family anymore, no.

Just the dogs looking through the glass doors from outside on their misty patio.

After what seemed like a long time, I was finally alone in Louise's house.

So quiet. Except for the occasional whimper from outside and Greta's dignified single scratch down the confining glass door.

I let the dogs in. They might as well know that their mother was gone.

Bruce jumped on me again, but only briefly, then he set off to sniff the house.

I sat on Louise's couch. It was all feeling familiar.

There was no view this time, the shades were all drawn. I had no desire to raise them.

I wasn't crying, it wasn't like that. I just sat in the cool house feeling numb.

I killed her.

I knew it. She was sick and I should have known.

I should have heard her coughing back in the restaurant and realized what it meant. She was too weak. She didn't want to tell me no. She wanted to help her friend.

But I should have stopped her when I saw the first sign that it was hurting. I let her go on instead.

I wanted what I wanted. I didn't care about anything else.

The dogs returned from their inspection. There was nothing I could say to them. I patted the couch beside me and Bruce took me up on my offer. He hopped up and dug at the cushion with his front paws before turning in a circle and plopping his chin onto my lap.

I rested my hand on his head. Greta stretched out on the floor at my feet.

The three of us sat like that for a long time.

At dusk some kind of internal clock seemed to go off

in both of them. They got up and began pacing in front of me.

I had a dog when I was growing up. It was always amazing how regular she was in knowing when it was time for her meals.

There was nothing for it. I couldn't just sit here. Louise's dogs deserved to eat. I let them out in case they needed it, then went into Louise's kitchen to search for their food.

I found it inside her pantry.

There was an envelope taped to the dog food bin.

In Louise's lovely handwriting: *LANEY.*

My hands shook as I slid my finger under the sealed flap and pulled out the two sheets of blue notebook paper inside.

Dearest Laney,

Please take care of my dogs. I know it's a lot to ask, but they're sweeter than anything and they will love you. I think you'll love them too.

I wrote out a will today, just in case. It's in the top drawer of my dresser. I talked to a lawyer a while ago and she said if I left a will in my own handwriting, it would be legal. I hope it works. You can have the house or you can sell it. I left you everything else too. Keep what you want or get rid of it. I only care about the dogs.

Don't be sad. This was going to happen anyway, and you probably saved me 6 months. I'd rather go helping you than just go.

I assume you got to talk to Danny. I hope it brought you comfort. He loved you. I only met him those few times, but I know that man absolutely loved you.

You asked me a long time ago why I do this for people, even people I don't know. I'm pretty sure I lied to you then. I said I felt it was my calling or something like that.

But the truth is it's not for them, it's for me. It's like being able

to watch the most fantastic series of movies. I get to see what death is like. I get to talk to the people who are there.
It's like I'm standing on a bridge between the living world and the dead. I've been standing here my whole life.

And now, if today goes the way I think it will, I'll just turn to my right and keep walking.

Kiss Greta and Bruce for me. They were the best thing about living on this side.

Thank you for being my friend. I wish we had more time, but we never do.

All my love, Louise

I stared at her note for a while longer, but then I could hear Bruce whining at the door.

I used the cup inside the dog food bin to measure out the amount that seemed right and filled the two dog bowls sitting empty on the kitchen floor. I let the dogs in. They rushed to their dinners. I watched them and thought about what to do.

It wasn't like with Danny. I could still think and move this time. Maybe if he had left me a note—*Laney, I knew I was going to die today. I'm sorry. I love you*—I would have felt the way I felt now. Sad, but not devastated. Sad, but not broken.

What did he really say? In all the flurry of what happened after, I hadn't had time to remember.

I wished I had recorded it. It was stupid I hadn't thought of that.

I didn't even take notes. Why? Didn't I know ahead of time that every word would be precious?

I leaned against Louise's chipped and stained kitchen counter and closed my eyes and tried hard to remember.

He said he wanted to be fearless.

He was.

That he loved me.

He did.

He was sorry to leave me so soon.

He did.

Skiing fearlessly across a snow bridge that held strong for everyone but him.

What was the point of it all? Of his short life, of meeting me, making me fall in love with him, marry him—what was the point if he wasn't going to stick around?

And there was Louise, standing on her own bridge, asking him exactly that question for me.

"What was the point, Danny?"

To love Laney. To make her happy.

He did. I can swear that he did.

The dogs were finished. I filled their bowls with water. They slurped it as ravenously as the food.

I crouched down and let Bruce overlick my face and I gave Greta's thick white neck a big hug.

What was the point of it all?

I was a widow with two dogs to take care of. With a friend's possessions to sort through and sell. With two houses now, if Louise's will was done right, and if she left me everything that probably meant a good deal of money too. Her mother was a wealthy woman when she died. Louise was her only child.

Whatever my future was now, it was completely different than the one I imagined just two weeks ago.

Or even two hours ago.

Bruce was bouncing from his back feet to his front now, yipping at me, excited.

Greta nudged my hand in her graceful way.

Too hot to walk. It was searing outside. But the dogs wanted what they wanted.

I took a few steps out of the kitchen toward the sliding glass door. I could tell by their reaction I'd gotten it right. I opened the door and went out on the patio. Bruce spun in a circle and took off.

He brought back one of the matted tennis balls and dropped it at my feet. He looked up at me expectantly, tail wagging like mad.

I threw it. Bruce ran out and retrieved it and brought it

back. We went on like that for about ten minutes while Greta stretched out on the cool concrete porch under the misters above and watched her crazy brother.

As I threw the tennis ball again, I could see it then, my life as this movie, reset into a brand new scene.

Standing on a bridge of my own now. Between my old life and the new.

I couldn't go left anymore, that path was closed to me now. My life with Danny was gone. What was the point of it all? Exactly what he said, exactly the words I could remember now: *To be alive. To love being alive. I wanted that and I got it.*

I was alive. Louise and Danny weren't anymore, but I was. And the two dogs, Greta and Bruce, they needed someone who was alive to love them and take care of them.

I could do that. For Louise, for Danny, for the dogs, for myself, I could do that.

I could do what Louise did. Turn right and keep on walking. Not into death, not now, not today, but into the unfamiliar world of a new and different life. Whatever it might look like. However long it might last.

A life without Danny, but still my life.

It was up to me to love it.

When it was finally too hot for Bruce to want to chase the ball anymore, the three of us went back inside.

I stood for a moment in Louise's living room, uncertain what to do next.

But then it was clear. Just take one step. I didn't have to know all of them, just take the next one.

I went in search of fresh sheets for Louise's bed. The dogs would want to sleep somewhere familiar tonight.

They were on this bridge with me too. They might as well get used to sleeping with me.

FROM THE BONES OF AN OLD DOG

INTRODUCTION

Tom Rubey's dog is gone. Hit by a car, and the driver never even stopped.

But maybe there is a way to get the dog back. To bring him back to life.

Maybe. If the story Tom heard is true.

Tom and his friend Billy Jane, the dog catcher's daughter, are willing to give it a try.

Even if it means believing in magic. And miracles. And the bones of an old dog.

A story of hope and bravery and the love of a good dog.

1

Tom Rubey knew it was probably a lie.

He wasn't stupid and he was a fair judge of character, so whenever Nathan Weaver said something Tom automatically only half listened.

Nathan knew about Tom's dog. The whole school did. How a truck ran over Rip and never even stopped to check. A rusted-out red truck, Billy Jane Culver said, left tail light busted, but she didn't see the driver, the truck was gone before she could look.

She ran out onto the street to see if poor Rip was still alive.

He lifted his golden head, whimpered, then his head dropped heavy back to the ground and Rip was dead.

Only seven. He still had at least seven more years left,

as far as Tom knew. Rip's dad Sargent lived till he was fourteen.

That was old for a big dog, the vet said at the time. Sargent had slowed down and his teeth were rotting and his back legs couldn't walk a straight line anymore, but he was still a good birder and he could give a shaky, palsy point. Labrador Retrievers aren't normally good pointers, but Sargent learned the skill on his own. Tom and his dad had good hunting with him almost all the way to the end.

Rip was already in the understudy position, bringing up the rear. He came out of Sargent's fourth stud litter, thirteen pups that time, and Tom got to pick out which one he wanted. Rip was the only one who looked Tom right in the eyes.

By the time Sargent died, Rip was in his prime. He could go all day, running up hillsides, chasing down doves across a mile of field, swimming across lakes to bring back ducks, you name it. Tom's dad said he might be an even better hunter than Sargent.

But Rip was mostly Tom's dog. He slept at the foot of Tom's bed every night, even though over time both Tom and Rip got bigger and there wasn't really room for them both. At some point during the night Tom would stretch out his legs in his sleep and Rip would jump down onto his dog bed on the floor, but both of them still started out every night together just like they did when Rip was a puppy.

And now after just seven years together, it was over.

After the red truck drove off, Billy Jane screamed out for people to help. They got Rip's body off to the side of Dutch's Frosty Stop Drive-In. One of the cooks brought out an armful of dish towels so they could cover him.

A crowd of kids gathered. But it was Billy Jane who took it upon herself to come running all the way to Tom's house to tell him Rip was dead and she saw it.

Rip's blood was still on her pale blue dress.

"I'm sorry, Tom," she said, bawling. She could barely get out the words. Finally she told him the whole story. Everything she saw.

"I don't think he suffered," Billy Jane said, but Tom could see in her eyes she wasn't being honest.

He didn't want to cry in front of her, he had always liked her, but something like this, it was hard to stay strong.

He cleared his throat instead, tried to seem like he was fine. But he had to swipe his hand across his cheeks several times.

"Thank you—" Clear his throat. "—thank you for telling me."

"Are you going to get his body?"

Tom nodded. He couldn't look Billy Jane in the eyes right then. He knew he'd start bawling too. They were both in the eighth grade. He was too old.

His dad was at work and his mom was visiting her

sister, so Tom had to find the supplies himself. He got a few green plastic lawn bags and a wheelbarrow. He just needed to get Rip home.

All the way back to Dutch's Frosty Stop, Billy Jane kept asking him if he was all right. Tom nodded every time, but he kept his head down so she wouldn't see.

He needed to cry so badly it felt like a tidal wave inside his throat.

He didn't want to look at Rip's body. He wished none of this was real.

There were still a bunch of kids hanging around Dutch's. Tom could see a kind of cruel eagerness on a few of their faces, Nathan Weaver's included, wondering if he was going to break down like a girl.

Tom tried to be like his dad. Very matter-of-fact about life and death. He was a carpenter and he'd been around a lot of job sites over the years, and men died of this and that and they just had to deal with it. Heart attack, accident on the site, truck accident on the way there. Things happened, life wasn't perfect. Tom's dad wasn't emotional about it, he understood that was the way things went.

If he was there with him now, Tom knew his father would be kind to old Rip and wouldn't be rough loading him into their car, but he also wouldn't act like it was the greatest tragedy in the world. Dogs died. When they woke up one morning and found old Sargent had died during the night, Tom's dad shook his head sadly and went out and dug a hole. He didn't cry about it, he just got on.

Tom cried, but he was much younger then. And his mother wept about it for days.

As Tom stood now next to Rip's outstretched body beneath all the towels, Billy Jane started crying again. She and a few of the other kids helped Tom cover Rip with the green plastic bags and then lift him onto the wheelbarrow.

Blood had soaked into the ground beneath where he'd been laying. A lump globbed in Tom's throat. He had to look away.

"Want help?" Randy Hudson asked him. He was one of Tom's best friends.

"Nah," Tom said as he picked up the two wooden handles of the wheelbarrow and found the balance point on the front wheel. "Thanks." He gave Randy a nod and pushed away from Dutch's Frosty Stop.

Billy Jane came with him.

She didn't talk much on the walk back. She kept watch on the plastic bags, and made sure to cover up Rip again any time they shifted.

But Tom kept catching glimpses of his dog. The yellow coat, his big goofy feet. A corner of one of his soft ears. This dog had been alive this morning. Tom knelt in front of him before school and scratched behind those ears the way he always did, and told Rip he'd see him later.

The dog hung out his tongue and wagged his thick yellow tail. And when Tom came home in the afternoons, Rip would be standing at the door waiting, tongue out, tail wagging.

Not today, though.

Tom pushed through the screen door, let it slam behind him, and expected to find Rip right there.

He knew the dog had his own life during the days. Dog friends to visit. Even a few businesses where they kept treats for Rip and some of the other regulars who stopped by.

People visiting from out of town sometimes reported them to the dog catcher. *Dangerous dogs roaming the streets!* Mr. Culver would nod very seriously, take down the report, then rip it up as soon as the stranger walked out.

Tom knew because Billy Jane was the dog catcher's daughter. She loved animals almost as much as Tom.

But something had gone wrong this time. Rip might have been on his way home to be there before Tom was back from school when the red truck with the busted tail light creamed him and kept on going.

Tom couldn't help it now. He sniffed back his runny nose and lifted his shoulder to try to wipe more tears off of his cheeks.

Billy Jane looked at him sideways and patted him on the back.

"It's terrible," she said softly. "I'm so sorry."

Tom let out a brief sound of grief and then stifled it and kept on pushing the wheelbarrow.

He had never appreciated Rip enough. A dog like that. Always looking for the fun. At Tom's side whenever it was time to go somewhere together, even if it was just up the block to visit Randy or one of the other kids. Rip trotted along with Tom as if any outing was an adventure. Then he'd lie on someone's porch while Tom played catch or threw around a football, and the minute Tom called him again he'd come running.

They fished together on Stilt's Pond in the little canoe Tom's dad helped him make. Rip would sit in the bow staring straight ahead, and whenever Tom caught a fish he held it out to Rip so the dog could give it a lick.

The dog was up for anything, always eager, always playful.

Never again. Tom still couldn't believe it.

Finally they reached his house. He rolled the wheelbarrow out back and set the metal legs down on the ground. He was sweating hard now, even though for May it wasn't that hot yet. Summer would be here soon, and in Macon, Missouri that meant humidity so thick the dogs and people alike could barely stand it.

Most of the kids went to the town pool every day, but

dogs weren't allowed. Tom took Rip out to the pond and let him dip in there, always with an eye out for snapping turtles and the poisonous water moccasins that hung around the water. On chore days when he didn't have that much time, the two of them just ran through the sprinklers.

But a day like today, sunny and not too hot, it would have been fun just to throw the ball to Rip in the back yard, then sit around in the shade and split a popsicle.

"Tom?" Billy Jane asked in a quiet voice. "What are you going to do now?"

Tom looked down at the lump covered in green plastic bags.

"Guess I'll dig a grave," he said.

Billy Jane nodded. She laid her hand on Tom's arm. "Want some company?"

"No." He looked up at her, met her tearful eyes. "Thanks."

Billy Jane made a sound like a small sob, then turned around and left.

Tom moved the wheelbarrow under the porch where Rip could have some shade.

Then he went off to the shed to get a shovel.

Out between the two maple trees in the back yard there was a wooden marker Tom's dad had made for Sargent. His dad was a good carver, but Tom wanted to make Rip's marker himself.

Tom helped his dad dig Sargent's grave, although he was younger then and didn't have much muscle. He remembered how hard it was, though, and how much longer it took than he ever expected.

He knew it would take him several hours to dig the hole all by himself, but he wanted to get started before his dad came home and offered to help. If Tom's hands were blistered by then, he might accept the help. But for now he wanted to do this for Rip on his own.

Now that no one could see him, he let the tears freely flow. They mingled with his sweat and dripped off his nose down into the turned-up soil.

It was hitting him now, the finality of it all. How one stupid careless truck driver could take away Rip's life. How quickly everything could change. How uncertain everything was.

Tom shoveled the dirt near to Sargent's grave, but far enough away that he wouldn't disturb the bones. Father and son lying close to each other, maybe still hunting if dogs had souls. Tom would never suggest that to his father, but he thought it nonetheless. What kind of world was it if a dog was just here for a few years and then died, and that was all he ever did? Why even bother creating dogs? There had to be more, especially with the kind of eagerness Rip brought to life. Of course dogs had souls.

Tom hoped Rip could see him now.

After an hour of constant digging, Tom heard his mother calling to him from the house.

He watched her come out, see the wheelbarrow, and then keep hurrying to Tom.

She took him into her arms. Tom laid his head against her chest. She was crying. She must have already heard. Word could always spread so fast.

"Oh, sweetheart," she said. "I'm so, so sorry. He was—" She choked on a sob. "—such a good dog!"

By now Tom had already cried out all his tears. "I know," was all he said. Then he pulled away to keep on digging.

"I'll bring you some lemonade," his mother said.

Tom nodded, but then thought better of it. "Can I have a popsicle instead?"

She brought him a cherry-flavored one, and he sat at the edge of the hole and took a break. When he was halfway through it he broke it in half and dropped it and the stick into the grave.

It felt right. As right as it could, considering how wrong this all was.

The day felt warmer now and he didn't want Rip to start to smell.

Tom got back to work and dug harder.

2

"Lord, we thank you for Rip," his mother said during grace.

"Amen," Tom and his father both muttered.

The digging went faster once Tom's dad got home.

They wheeled Rip out to the grave and between them gently lowered him into the hole.

Tom wanted to shovel the dirt back in by himself. His dad gave him a nod of approval and went back in the house.

That night Tom put off going to bed. He sat in the living room, he sat at the stiff uncomfortable chair at the kitchen table, he sat and walked around until he knew he was tired enough to sleep.

Still, when he lay down between the sheets, the bed was too large and his legs stretched out too early. He lay awake thinking of Rip alone in the lonely hole. Close to Sargent, but not really together.

It was morbid, thinking of their two dead bodies, but it was all he could imagine as he finally fell into sleep.

The next day was Saturday, and Tom went about his chores with a kind of numb mechanical process. Mow the grass, wash the car, clean his room, weed the yard.

He talked to Rip in his mind, describing everything he was doing, telling him what a good dog he had been and how he wished they could go to the pond or down to Randy's house or over to Billy Jane's, where they never went, but now Tom wished maybe they could.

Billy Jane would have petted Rip's head and talked to him in that kind of baby talk girls used that always sounded so ridiculous, but dogs always loved it. Billy Jane was good with dogs. She'd go help her dad at the pound on Saturdays and take the dogs out of their cages and walk them. She helped put up fliers to find their owners. Tom listened to Billy Jane and her friends talk about it sometimes. She said the vet told her when she was older she could come work over there.

On Sunday Tom and his parents went to church.

Nathan Weaver's father was the pastor. Proving that just because you're a pastor's kid, that doesn't make you good. Nathan was a liar and a bully and a show-off. Maybe he thought he could get away with it because of who his father was, and it seemed to work with the grown-ups, since they never wanted to believe how bad he really was, but the kids all knew it and everyone stayed away from him. Nathan was a jerk.

He liked to brag about all the important people who came to visit them at their house. Preachers from bigger towns, missionaries who had been to Africa, even a famous gospel singer once whose car had broken down in Macon on her way to a bigger church in Kirksville.

This Sunday was no different.

"He taught me some words in Swahili," Nathan was telling some of the boys. He said a few words that sounded invented. "He just came back from the Congo. He's staying with us the next two days."

Tom looked over where Nathan was indicating, to a stooped-over very thin man who looked too old to have survived in the jungle. He was clutching a very worn-out Bible to his chest and nodding piously to one of the old ladies from the choir.

Tom could hear her say, "Bless you," as she gave his thin arm a squeeze. The thin man moved on to another group of people.

"He's taking a collection," Nathan informed his reluctant audience. "He's going all over Missouri for the next four weeks. Then he'll use the money to go back and build a school."

Sure enough, Tom saw Pastor Weaver following along

after the missionary with a collection plate that was already full of quarters and dollar bills.

"You should hear him, Tom," Nathan said, suddenly turning in his direction. "He told us the strangest story last night."

Tom hated to give Nathan Weaver even an ounce of attention, but Nathan didn't usually single any of them out. He only wanted to talk about himself. Sometimes it was as if he pretended he didn't even know anyone else's name.

"He said he was witnessing to a group of natives about Jesus being resurrected. They got all excited and told him through an interpreter that they already knew."

"Knew what?" Tom asked with barely-masked hostility. He still remembered the look on Nathan's face when Tom came to carry away Rip's body. That kind of wicked satisfaction some people take in another person's disaster.

"About resurrection," Nathan said. "Their healing man had raised lots of people from the dead."

This, finally, was of interest to the crowd. A lot of heads turned in Nathan's direction. He smiled at the new popularity. He milked his story as much as he could.

"Yeah, they said he had just saved a little baby a few days before. The parents had already buried it, but the healer had them dig it up again and he brought it back to life."

A chill swept up Tom's spine.

But Nathan was a liar. He couldn't fall for this.

"How?" Randy Hudson asked. A lot of the other kids voiced the same question.

Nathan drew himself up. He was a big man now. The undisputed center of attention.

"You want to know how?" Nathan asked them.

Kids nodded.

"You really want to know?"

"Come on," Tom said angrily. This was getting ridiculous.

Nathan grinned at him. "Bet you want to do it for your dog."

"Shut up," Billy Jane said. Tom hadn't seen her come over. She was wearing a yellow dress with a bright white collar, a flowery straw hat, and white gloves like the other girls wore to church in the spring.

There was a large group of kids around now, and more and more were joining.

Nathan must have had some realization just then, because he looked around nervously for his father. Pastor Weaver was at the far end of the church, still chatting with his congregation and collecting their donations.

Nathan motioned for the crowd to draw in closer.

Normally Tom would have resisted, but this time he couldn't.

Nathan continued in a quieter voice. "He told the parents to go dig up the body of one of their ancestors."

"Ew," one of the girls said.

A few of the boys rolled their eyes.

"Then grind up the bones," Nathan said, "and put them inside a pot with a hole in the lid. You dig a hole that's big enough for the pot, and put a jar or some other kind of container in the bottom of it. Then you turn the pot upside down so the hole in the lid is right on top of the jar."

"I don't believe any of this," Randy Hudson said. "You're just making it all up."

Tom appreciated his friend for saying it.

"It's too complicated," one of the other boys said.

Nathan made a *psshi*ng sound. "You're bringing back somebody from the dead. You think that's supposed to be easy?"

That seemed to settle down the rest of the skeptics.

"So the pot is upside down in a hole," Nathan continued, "and the hole in the lid is on top of the jar. You got that?"

His listeners nodded.

"Then you put wood all around the pot. You make a big fire and you keep feeding it more wood all night."

"Like making a stew?" one of the girls asked.

"No, stupid," Nathan said. "Did I say there was any water in there? It's just the bones."

The girl blushed. Tom hated Nathan all the more for it.

"So what?" Tom said. "You're burning a bunch of bones. Probably smells bad, but they're just burnt bones."

"Shows what you know," Nathan said with the kind of arrogance Tom was used to. "The bones melt into *tar*."

Tom and Randy exchanged a look. Neither of them really knew enough to argue.

"Then the tar drips into the jar beneath the pot, understand?" Nathan said. "That tar is what you use."

Billy Jane stood protectively in front of the girl Nathan had called stupid. She held her head high, chin on the level. She wasn't going to be pushed around.

"I've never heard of any of that," she said. "Randy's right, it sounds made up."

"Why would you have heard of it?" Nathan said. "It's from the *Congo*. You've never been outside Macon."

Billy Jane frowned, but she didn't argue.

And Tom had to admit to himself, he was still listening.

"So then what?" Tom asked.

Nathan's smile was far too triumphant. He knew he had Tom dangling from his hook. Tom hated it, but he had to know.

"The healer poured the tar on the grave of their dead baby. He said whatever spell they use there. The missionary told the parents they shouldn't have done that, it might be praying to the devil, but they said the healer only ever prayed to their gods. The healer told them to come back and check the grave in the morning."

Nathan paused, looking around at his audience and relishing their suspense.

But Tom wouldn't be the one to break it.

"Well?" Billy Jane said. She crossed her arms over her chest.

Nathan imitated the sound of a crying baby.

Kids gasped. *"No."*

Nathan smiled and nodded. "Yes. Good as new."

A kind of awed silence overtook the group. Kids looked from one to another.

Billy Jane caught Tom's eye. She looked skeptical, but she shrugged.

As if to say, *It might be worth a try.*

3

Tom waited for Nathan to come out of church. Waited for him to be alone with just his folks. Even better, Pastor and Mrs. Weaver were busy talking to the missionary, so for the moment, Nathan was alone.

Tom motioned him aside. Again, that triumphant look on Nathan's face. But Tom had to ignore it.

"What words did the healer say?" he asked.

"They were in Swahili," Nathan said in that sarcastic tone that made Tom want to punch his rabbity face.

Tom took a breath and maintained his calm. "But what did they *mean*," he asked.

"I don't know," Nathan said. "Ask him." He pointed to the stooped-over missionary.

There was an ugly tilt to Nathan's lip, as if daring Tom to go get in trouble.

But if any of that story was true, Tom was willing to take the risk.

He waited until there was a break in the conversation among the grown-ups, then he quickly approached the missionary.

"Excuse me, sir. Can I ask you a question?"

The missionary squinted at Tom like a man who needed glasses, but he smiled in an encouraging way. "Of course, young man. Ask away."

Tom cleared his throat. "My friend..." He pointed at Nathan who was avidly watching from a short distance away. "He said you told them a story last night about a healer and a baby who died."

"Ah, yes," the missionary said. A wistful look passed over his face. "Poor couple. They were very upset. But then all ended well, eh?"

Tom's heart picked up pace. "Then it's true? He really saved the baby?"

"I tend to think the couple was mistaken," the missionary said. "The baby might have been sick, but more likely unconscious than dead. But then..." The missionary lifted his thin shoulders. "The Lord does raise the dead occasionally, doesn't he? Lazarus, the centurion's servant, have you read your Bible, son?"

"Yes, sir," Tom answered, and the truth was on his side. Every Christmas Eve his mother liked him to read out loud the story of Jesus's birth.

"Then you know," the missionary said. "All believers will one day be resurrected. It's the promise of our Lord."

"But how did the healer do it?" Tom persisted. "Do you have any idea what words he said?"

The missionary gazed at Tom with a pitying kind of look. "They're heathens, you understand."

"Yes, sir," Tom said impatiently.

"That's why the Lord sent me there, to bring them into his fold."

"Yes, sir, I understand," Tom said. "But still..." He cast around for a better idea. "I'm doing a Sunday School report. I want to talk about you and the work you're doing. But I need to give them all the facts. So, if you remember what he said..."

"No, young man, I'm sorry," the missionary said. "I only know the Lord's words by heart."

4

Tom trudged along home with his parents. They lived just a few blocks from the church and when the weather was nice they always walked.

He was surprised to hear footsteps running behind him. Even more surprised to see Billy Jane.

"Hi, Mr. and Mrs. Robey," she said.

Tom's parents greeted her, then Tom saw his mother give his father a look.

"We'll see you at home," she said, smiling at Tom. She murmured something to Tom's father, then tugged on his arm to keep on walking.

As soon as they were alone, Billy Jane got right to the point. "Do you believe it?"

Tom didn't have to ask her what.

"I don't know," he said.

"I do," said Billy Jane. "I saw something like that in a book."

Billy Jane was the biggest reader Tom knew. She loved books almost as much as animals. Every Saturday she checked out the maximum number of books from the Macon library, and she read them all by the following Saturday when she checked out more.

"Let's go after school tomorrow," she said. "I'll find it again."

5

Tom felt foolish doing it, in case it was all an elaborate hoax, but he spent time looking through his mother's cookware for some kind of a pot with a hole in the lid.

There was the pressure cooker she used for canning when she made jam, but she'd skin him alive if she found out he cooked Sargent's bones in it.

If he was even going to do this. It sounded so far-fetched, he constantly talked himself out of it. Would he really dig up their old dead dog? What if it there was still flesh on his bones? He had been dead several years now, but Tom had no idea how quickly a body decomposed. He might open up the grave and find maggots and a half-eaten corpse. What if it smelled like rotting meat? His mother would be horrified at what he'd done.

By the time Tom went to bed, he wasn't sure what he would do, but he was still no closer to finding the kind of pot Nathan described.

By the next afternoon, it seemed he wouldn't need it.

Billy Jane walked through the library with the kind of ownership Tom felt toward Stilt's Pond. Complete familiarity, the confidence of knowing exactly what to do and where to go. Soon she had searched through the card catalog and remembered which book she wanted.

"It's about a Russian pilgrim," she whispered as they went to the relevant shelf.

"Why would you read that?" Tom asked.

Billy Jane gave him a look as if it was obvious. "I'm going to read every book in here."

Tom gazed at her in wonder. It was like saying she was going to fish in every body of water in the state, everything from puddles up to lakes.

The two of them sat at a table far in the back and opened the old tattered book.

Billy Jane flipped through the pages, searching for the passage. Once she found it, she pressed her finger to the paragraph as she passed the book to Tom.

He read it, then read it again.

The process was almost exactly the way Nathan described.

That alone worried him.

"What if Nathan read this book?" he asked. "And just said it was what the missionary told him?"

Billy Jane scoffed. "Mrs. Linn told me no one has checked this out in at least thirty years. Sometimes I'm the only person who has checked out a book *ever*."

Mrs. Linn was the librarian, and obviously a reliable source.

Tom read through the paragraph a third time. Billy Jane got up briefly and returned with a slip of paper and a short yellow pencil. She copied down the words from the book. Then she smiled at Tom and handed him the slip of paper and said, "I want to be there when you do it."

6

___

The Russian pilgrim used a different kind of pot. He described it as *earthen*, and Billy Jane pointed out that a flower pot would be perfect. "It has a hole in the bottom. And we can put foil over the top to keep it covered."

Tom always knew she was smart. But it wasn't just good grades. She had more ideas every five minutes than he could come up with in a whole day.

He found several unused flower pots out in the shed. He and Billy Jane looked them over, wondering what size they needed.

"Do you think you should use *all* of the bones?" she asked.

"Probably," Tom said. In the book the pilgrim used all

sorts of different animal bones, from bird bones to whatever other kinds he could find in the forest.

Billy Jane pointed at the largest pot. "Then we'll probably need that one."

"That's a big hole to dig," said Tom, who had recent experience to draw from.

Instead he chose one of the medium-sized pots. "Remember, we have to grind the bones anyway," Tom said. "That will take up less room."

It was going to be a long, maybe difficult process.

But the fact that Billy Jane wanted to do it with him made it a lot easier.

"Should we do it tonight?" she asked, almost in a whisper.

"Why not?" Tom said. If it worked, he wanted Rip back alive as soon as possible.

If it worked.

He still wasn't sure that this whole thing was real. Even the Russian pilgrim might have been lying. Just because something was in a book didn't make it true.

And he could just see Nathan Weaver laughing at him if he ever found out. Telling all the kids at school how gullible Tom was. *"You actually dug up your old dead dog? That's disgusting!"*

But Billy Jane believed it. And that gave Tom a certain amount of faith.

It was Monday, a school night, so Billy Jane wouldn't

be able to stay too long. She told her parents she was having dinner with the Robeys, which was true. Tom's mother was only too happy to include Billy Jane at dinner. She switched from leftovers to spaghetti and meatballs since they had a guest.

Tom's mother kept shooting his father significant looks all during dinner, but Tom forced himself to ignore them. His plans were too important to worry about his mother getting the wrong idea. He would explain to her later that Billy Jane was just a friend.

It was still light out after dinner. The sun wasn't going to set until nearly 8:30. Billy Jane's mother wanted her home before then.

"So you'll walk me home," Billy Jane told him, "and then I'll pretend to go to bed, and I'll come right back."

"I don't want you to get into trouble."

"I won't," she said. "My parents sleep like they're dead. They'll never find out."

For now, by the light of the yellow and orange sunset, they walked out to the two maple trees and surveyed where they would dig.

Billy Jane said she would use one of the shovels too. She'd helped her dad in the yard before.

"We have to do it quietly," Tom told her. "I can't let my parents hear."

"Tell them you remembered you wanted to put Rip's

favorite toy in his grave," Billy Jane said. "You have to do it tonight or you'll never sleep."

"Yeah ... okay," Tom said. He was amazed at how Billy Jane's mind worked. "Then we'll both dig at the same time so they only hear the sound of one shovel."

"Good idea," Billy Jane said. Tom appreciated the praise.

They brought out the flower pot and set it in position. To grind the bones Tom had a large smooth rock that fit neatly in his hand. Billy Jane would break up the bones with the blade of a garden trowel, and Tom would do the grinding.

They carried over logs from the woodpile and gathered dry twigs and old newspapers out of the trash to act as tinder.

The two of them stood back to examine their work.

Billy Jane looked up at the darkening sky. "You should walk me home now. I'll go say goodbye to your parents."

She thanked Tom's mother for the delicious dinner. Tom could see how much his mother liked that.

As Tom left to walk Billy Jane home he could hear his parents softly laughing.

7

It was close to ten o'clock before Billy Jane came back. By then Tom had dug down to the top of Sargent's bones. He stopped digging as soon as his shovel hit something hard. He wanted to leave some of the shoveling to Billy Jane if she still wanted to.

But just to make sure, he bent down and brushed away some of the dirt in case it was something he didn't want Billy Jane to have to see. To his relief there was no rotting, decomposing meat. Just bare bones that looked yellow under the glow of the full moon.

Tom watched Billy Jane's flashlight beam grow closer.

"Hi," she whispered.

"Hi."

She was wearing jeans and sneakers and a dark cotton

blouse. Her hair was back in a headband, ready for her to work.

"Sorry I'm so late," Billy Jane whispered. "I'm glad you got started."

Tom showed her the first of the bones. He finished uncovering it and pulled it out of the dirt. It was about a foot long and might have belonged to a leg.

Billy Jane looked a little nervous as he held it in front of her. She leaned forward and sniffed it. It seemed like a good idea. Tom did the same.

It smelled a little like one of the beef bones he used to give Rip to chew, still full of marrow he'd spend hours working out with his tongue.

This bone was hard and thick like that. Not brittle and easy to break.

Not at all the way it sounded like in the Russian pilgrim's book.

Tom mentioned that to Billy Jane. She thought about it for a moment.

"The pilgrim found all those bones already on top of the ground in the forest," she said. "Maybe they were already brittle because they were exposed to the air."

Tom tried to crack the bone apart first with the garden trowel, then with his larger shovel. But it was like trying to break open a walnut with the tip of a pencil. The bone wasn't even close to fragile enough that Tom would be able to chop it up in smaller pieces and then grind it.

He sat back on his heels, discouraged.

"So we won't use all the bones," Billy Jane said. "Just a few of them. And that way we can use one of the smaller pots. Come on, we can still do this." She tugged on his sleeve and started for the shed.

Tom appreciated her optimism. He didn't want to give up, either. If there was even the slightest possibility that what the missionary and the Russian pilgrim both said was true, Tom absolutely wanted to try.

They picked out the only small pot that wasn't cracked and brought it back to the grave. Tom already had a big section of foil he'd gotten from his mother's kitchen drawer. He folded it up smaller to fit the rim of the substitute pot.

Then he and Billy Jane picked out the bones that they would burn.

"That thick one will take too long," he said. "It's like a Yule log."

In the pilgrim book, the ground-up bones burned down to an oily reddish-black tar in twenty-four hours.

Tom doubted that he had twenty-four hours. He couldn't keep the fire burning while he was at school. At most he could hope the coals would keep the flower pot hot for a few extra hours after he stopped adding wood.

At last everything was in place: one of his mother's canning jars down at the bottom of the hole, the flower pot sitting on top of it, a collection of small bones inside it, and the foil tightly covering the top.

He balled up the newspapers and set twigs all around and lit a match.

He and Billy Jane squatted near the little fire and took turns adding more tinder. Before long the flames were circled all around the pot.

"Tom?" his mother's voice called from the back of the house.

"Hide!" Tom whispered.

Billy Jane was already ducking behind one of the maples when Tom's mother started across the yard.

"What ever are you doing?" she asked.

He jumped to his feet and hurried forward to meet her.

The words leapt to his tongue. "I decided I'd like to sleep out here tonight," he said. "Please, Mom. Just this once. I just want to say goodbye to Rip."

"Oh, honey." She reached out and ran her fingers through the top of his hair. Tom cringed at the gesture. It was something she used to do when he was a little kid.

Not something he wanted Billy Jane to see. Like his mother still treated him like a baby.

"Please, Mom," he said again.

"It's a school night," she said.

"I know, but I can't sleep without him yet. I know I'll be able to sleep if I stay out here."

He could see her hesitating. His mother had a soft heart, especially where animals were concerned.

"You promise you won't stay up all night?" she asked.

"Promise."

She set one hand on her hip. "All right, but just tonight. You run in and get your sleeping bag and a pillow. You can't sleep on the bare ground."

Tom didn't wait for more discussion. He ran into the house, knowing Billy Jane would stay hidden behind the tree.

He pulled his rolled-up sleeping bag off the upper shelf in his closet and took his pillow off the bed. His mother was waiting for him when he got back to the kitchen. She held out a flashlight, which he was glad to take. He didn't realize he'd want one until Billy Jane showed up with hers.

"Thanks, Mom."

She patted his shoulder and he ran back outside to the fire. It was time to feed it more wood.

8

Around eleven, Billy Jane was having a hard time staying awake.

She lay down on the dirt with her hands folded underneath her cheek. Tom debated whether to offer her his pillow. It might not smell very good, since he sometimes drooled on it during the night. He'd hate for her to smell it and think he was disgusting.

What he really needed to do was walk her home. Even though he wanted her company. But he couldn't have her staying out until midnight. What if her parents woke up after all and found that she was gone?

He gently rocked her shoulder.

She sat up and brushed the dirt from her hair.

"I should walk you home now," Tom said.

Billy Jane didn't argue.

She opened the corner of the foil to take a peek inside. Tom looked, too.

A meaty-smelling smoke escaped from the top. The bones looked like they might be softening.

It was interesting, in a way, but then he remembered these weren't just any bones, they once belonged to Sargent. And that made him think of Rip, lying dead in the nearby grave.

He smoothed the foil back over the top.

They added a few more pieces of wood to burn while Tom was away. Then they set out by moonlight and flashlight to walk the block and a half to Billy Jane's house.

She led him around to the side where three steps climbed up to the door.

"Good luck," she whispered. "I'll come over before school tomorrow. Wait for me."

She gave his hand a squeeze and ran up the steps.

All the way home Tom thought about that squeeze. What it meant. If anything.

Was it just a friendly gesture? Or was it her way of saying she liked him?

Or was it just that she was enthusiastic about their project? She would have squeezed even Nathan Weaver's hand out of excitement.

Tom returned to tending his fire. He stirred the orange coals with a stick, then added a few thin logs.

Then he unrolled his sleeping bag and set his pillow

on top and crawled inside. He might take a little nap for a while and get up in an hour or so to add more wood.

Birdsong woke him.

The fire had burned out, but the ashes were still warm. The flower pot was cool enough to touch.

He tilted it to the side to check the canning jar below.

A thin smear of dark liquid covered the glass bottom.

Tom grinned.

He checked the bones in the pot. There were still solid-looking, but much whiter than they seemed by moonlight last night.

Billy Jane arrived while he was examining them.

She looked fresh and clean in her plaid skirt, white blouse, rolled-down white bobby socks, and penny loafers. She wore her shoulder-length brown hair pulled back in a headband. He bet her breath smelled like toothpaste.

Tom hadn't even been inside his house yet to wash up. He probably smelled like smoke and bad breath. So he kept a certain distance, but he was still anxious to show Billy Jane what was in the jar.

She laughed and looked at him bright-eyed. "It worked!"

He put the jar back under the pot and added small pieces of wood around it to stoke up the fire again. "I'm going to let it burn the whole twenty-four hours and get as much liquid as we can."

"Good," said Billy Jane. "Then we can do the rest of it tonight."

The rest of it.

Pouring it over Rip's grave and bringing that good dog back to life.

9

Tom's mother wouldn't let him sleep outside again. He had to sneak out after his parents went to bed.

He realized it wasn't right for Billy Jane to walk to his house alone, so he told her after school to wait for him this time.

She told him which window was her bedroom. It was after eleven when he tapped on it.

She came bounding down the steps just a few minutes later. They set off quickly for Tom's house.

"Did you check it?" she asked.

"Not yet," he said. "I thought we could look together."

He'd added more wood all afternoon once he got home from school.

"What are you burning out there?" his mother asked.

"Rip's toys," he lied.

His mother looked at him strangely.

"Billy Jane said the vet told her about it. He said it helps get over the loss of a pet."

Tom's mother got a sad look in her eyes. He hated to lie to her, but he had to do it.

"I miss him, too," she said. Her eyes were misting up. She reached over to run her fingers through Tom's hair, but he dodged her in time.

"I'll be done tonight," Tom said. "Then I can really say goodbye."

What was he going to tell her if Rip suddenly sprang back to life? How was he going to explain?

He would worry about that later.

Right now he just hoped with all his heart that it worked.

When they checked the jar, there was about half an inch of a foul-smelling liquid. It looked thick enough to qualify as tar.

"Okay," Tom said, his voice breathier than normal. He could feel his heartbeat starting to race.

Billy Jane reached over and squeezed his hand again. He smiled at her and she nervously smiled back.

Tom wasn't nervous. He felt brave. Brave and ready to do what came next.

He pulled out of his pocket the slip of paper Billy Jane

had written on in the library. He had read it so many times since then, he could probably say the words from memory, but this was too important to leave to chance.

They moved over to Rip's grave. The dirt on top looked darker and looser than Sargent's older grave.

Tom scooped down through the top of the soil and made a little well.

Billy Jane held the jar poised over the grave, ready for Tom to say the words.

He cleared his throat.

"Love of creation," he began. "O create. Love of living. O give life."

The words were strange, but the Russian pilgrim lived a long time ago, and maybe they talked that way.

"Life shall ever have dominion over death," he went on, "and the pure in heart shall know Thee by your hand."

Billy Jane waited, wide-eyed. Her hand looked frozen where it held the jar.

Tom nodded to her solemnly.

Billy Jane gently tipped out the liquid.

It flowed thick like fudge over a sundae. Billy Jane shook out the last few drops.

Then Tom folded the loose dirt over the top of it, filling in the well.

The two of them knelt beside the grave and waited.

Tom was afraid to breathe.

The light from the full moon had been shining down on their ceremony up to now, but an instant later a cloud moved across it and shrouded them in darkness.

"Tom?" Billy Jane whispered.

He continued holding his breath and couldn't answer.

He felt her hand clasping his. That was fine. He held on and waited for what would happen.

A strong wind blew toward them from his house with enough power to ruffle Tom's hair. Loose dirt from the top of Rip's grave gusted into the air.

Billy Jane gave a little yelp and held on tighter.

The wind gathered around Tom and Billy Jane and the graves like they were at the center of a spinning carnival ride.

Tom closed his eyes.

He thought he could feel something brushing lightly against his arms.

A slight weight on top of his thighs.

The soft squirming of a small furry body.

The milk-sour smell of a puppy's breath.

Tom gasped and opened his eyes.

He could have sworn he saw a shape made of smoke.

He turned to Billy Jane, but she was staring straight ahead to exactly where Tom had been looking a moment before.

"Did you see it?" she whispered.

Tom's heart pounded.

"See what?" He needed to make sure.

Billy Jane released Tom's hand and pantomimed the size and shape.

"A puppy," she whispered in awe.

Tom swallowed hard. "Yeah. I think I saw it."

The wind curdled around them one last time, and then it died as quickly as it rose.

The cloud moved aside, and the moon shone brightly once more.

Tom and Billy Jane looked at each other.

Then they both looked at Rip's grave.

Tom expected to see the dirt bursting up as Rip dug himself to the surface.

But they waited. And waited.

At last Tom couldn't stand it. He got the shovel and dug down himself.

If Rip was alive but too buried in dirt, maybe it was up to Tom to free him.

But once he dug deep enough, he knew he was close to Rip's body.

He couldn't stand hitting him with the blade of the shovel. Instead he knelt beside the hole and called.

"Rip? Rip boy?"

"Rip," Billy Jane joined in.

There was a break in her voice. In another moment, she was crying.

"I thought it worked," she said.

"So did I," Tom answered. He felt a horrible pain in his chest.

They waited a little while longer. Billy Jane cried until it was time to walk her home.

10

Tom moved through the day in a sort of daze, unsure if what he thought happened last night really did.

The shape made out of smoke. The feeling of soft fur and the warm weight of a small living body.

The irresistible smell of a puppy's breath.

Had it all been in his head?

But it was in Billy Jane's head, too, or else it really did happen the way they both saw it. They ate their sandwiches outside together at lunch so they could go over it several more times.

They each took turns describing exactly what they remembered.

When Tom described holding the puppy, Billy Jane's eyes teared up again.

"I wish I could have felt that," she said. "But I saw it, and I swear I could hear it panting."

"Do you think we scared it away?" Tom said. He couldn't remember making any fast motions, but he might have forgotten.

Billy Jane shook her head. "We were both as still as statues. Once the wind started, I don't think either of us ever moved."

"Then what do you think it all was?" Tom asked. "Why didn't Rip come back?"

Billy Jane sighed. "We must have gotten it only half right. We're such amateurs. I bet a real Congo healer could have done it."

It wasn't the answer Tom wanted. He needed to fix this now.

"I think we should try again," he said. "Start over and do it again."

Billy Jane crumpled her sandwich paper and got up from the low seat wall in the back of the school.

"I agree," she said. "We got so close. I know we can do it next time."

"But what *was* it?" Tom asked again as they walked together back inside.

She suddenly stopped and clutched his arm. "Oh my gosh, that's it."

She softly repeated the familiar sound they'd both heard Nathan Weaver make a few days before.

The crying sound of a baby.

"Maybe they all start over," she said. "Whether they're a baby or an adult." She smiled, sure she had the answer. "Rip isn't coming back like he was, he's coming back as a *puppy*."

11

As they walked down Vine Street after school, making plans for how to do it right this time, Billy Jane suddenly drew in a sharp breath.

She pointed to the street.

"Tom, that's him."

A rusted red truck with a busted left tail light was turning right into the parking lot of the Bungalow Café.

A red mist seemed to cloud Tom's eyes.

A flash of hatred overtook his mind.

He took off at a run. Billy Jane called to him, then started running too.

He was down the block and across the street so fast it was like some sprinter had possessed his body.

"Tom! Tom!" Billy Jane cried. "What are you going to do?"

He didn't answer because he didn't know. He stood in the parking lot for a moment to catch his breath, then opened the door to the Bungalow Café and went inside.

He didn't get a good look at the man when he left his truck, other than to notice he wore a dark shirt.

Tom scanned the people on the stools at the counter, then looked to his left at the row of booths.

A loud laugh reached his ears. Something about the sound of that voice made him hurt. He found the dark-shirted man sitting with two friends in the second-to-last booth.

Billy Jane caught Tom's arm. "Those men are big," she warned him.

Tom didn't care. Right was right. He strode fearlessly to the booth.

"Is that your red truck?" he asked the laughing man.

The man wasn't laughing now.

"What if it is?" he said.

"Then mister, you killed my dog."

Conversations stopped. Tom's voice had come out louder than he expected. But he didn't care, he stood his ground. Hatred steeled his spine.

The man looked about Tom's parents' age. He had black hair slicked back from his forehead. He wore tan workpants and a plaid short-sleeved, button-down shirt. His arms looked tan and muscular like maybe he worked on machinery or did some other kind of physical labor.

He sat alone on his side of the booth. Now he scooted to the end and stood up.

He was at least a foot taller than Tom. But Tom stared him down like they were the same size.

People in the café were watching.

The man seemed to notice that too.

"Come talk to me outside," he said to Tom.

Without waiting for agreement, the man headed for the door.

"No, Tom," Billy Jane pleaded as he passed her. "Please don't get in a fight."

Tom had only been in one fight ever before, and that was when he was eight.

It was a lot of pushing and rolling around. Neither of them threw a punch.

He didn't know what the red truck man would do. If it was a real fight, Tom knew he would lose.

But to just drive over someone's dog and not even stop.

To kill Rip and not even care.

If Tom didn't stand up for something like that, he'd feel like a coward the rest of his life.

He only hoped the man wouldn't hit him too hard.

And that he could hit the man hard enough himself.

The man stood waiting at the side of the red truck.

"What's your name, boy?"

Tom glared at him. He didn't have to answer.

"I'm Ray Swadley," the man said, sticking out his hand.

People were coming out of the café to watch. Including Ray Swadley's two mean-looking friends.

Billy Jane was watching too. She stood with her hands clasped together in front of her mouth. Her eyes were wide with fright.

Ray lowered his outstretched hand. He glanced over at the crowd and then turned his back to them.

"When was this?" he said.

For a moment Tom didn't understand what he was asking.

"Friday," Tom said.

Ray Swadley gave a heavy sigh.

He looked back toward his two friends, then faced Tom again and reached into his back pocket. He pulled out his wallet.

"Look, I'm real sorry," he said. "But it wasn't me. Someone borrowed my truck."

He pulled out a ten-dollar bill and handed it to Tom.

Tom had no desire to take it.

Ray Swadley sighed again. He added another ten.

When Tom made no move to take them, Ray pushed them into his palm.

"I've got a dog," Ray said. "So I know. I'm real sorry. Nothing else I can do."

He went to pat Tom's shoulder, but Tom flinched away.

The anger had no place to go. It was still a hurricane inside his head.

Money was no substitute for a dog. Money was no apology for death.

That was what he wanted, Tom realized. Something more than just *I'm real sorry*.

"Do you even care?" he asked Ray Swadley as the man headed back to eat with his friends.

"I got my own problems," Ray said. "They're a lot bigger than yours."

The crowd wandered back inside, clearly disappointed there wasn't a fight.

Billy Jane looked wilted and tired. She came over as soon as Ray left.

Tears shone in her eyes. "I'm proud of you."

The tension started to make itself known in Tom's body. He could feel his hands and legs shake.

He nodded, not trusting his voice not to shake too.

He turned back toward Vine and walked hard.

"How much did he give you?" Billy Jane asked in a while.

Tom showed her the two ten-dollar bills still stuffed in his hand.

Billy Jane made a *pfff* of disapproval. He glanced at her. She was all right.

By the time they got back to Tom's house, he felt as dry and depleted as a husk. He greeted his mother and invited Billy Jane to take a seat while he got out two glasses and the pitcher of lemonade.

"How was school today?" his mother asked.

Tom and Billy Jane exchanged a look.

"Fine," Tom said.

"Good," Billy Jane answered.

The two of them sat at the kitchen table and drained their glasses.

"Oh, Tom," his mother said, "I wanted to tell you. I was talking to Mrs. Doughty today. You'll never guess."

The Doughtys lived out on five acres at the west end of town. Their daughter Beth was a year younger than Tom.

"Their dog Sadie just had a litter."

Tom jerked his head up, alert.

Billy Jane sat up straight. "What kind?"

"Labrador Retriever, same as Rip."

Tom was out of his chair in a flash.

"If you wait till your dad gets home, he can drive you," his mother said.

"That's all right," Tom said. Billy Jane was close at his heels.

"Be home for supper," his mother called, but Tom and Billy Jane were already running.

12

Mrs. Doughty was a stout, friendly woman with thick rough hands. Her daughter Beth looked like she'd grow up to be just the same.

"Eight of 'em are already spoken for," Mrs. Doughty said. "But there's still that little girl over there and one of those boys rolling in the grass."

All of the puppies were black. Some explored the vast backyard on their own, while two of them tumbled and played with each other near a rose bush close to the house. Their bright white teeth flashed as they growled in mock fight.

Billy Jane was already sitting cross-legged on the lawn, holding the girl puppy Mrs. Doughty pointed out. Soon Beth Doughty came out to join her.

Billy Jane lifted the puppy to her face and rubbed her

cheek against the soft fur. The girl dog bit the tip of her nose. Billy Jane laughed.

"Aww, I wish I could have one!" she said.

"Your daddy lets you keep dogs," Beth said.

"I know, but he says we already have too many animals," Billy Jane said with a sigh. "But just one more! She's so sweet."

"It's the smaller one," Mrs. Doughty said to Tom as he headed over to the wrestling puppies. "The bigger one's going to Jed Jepson."

Tom extracted the smaller of the two boys and turned him around to look at his face.

The dog looked directly into his eyes.

A lump sprang into Tom's throat.

He sat on the grass and held the puppy on his lap. And knew in the instant that he had done this before.

Not just with Rip seven years ago, but with a puppy made of smoke last night.

Tom closed his eyes. He could smell the puppy's milk-sour breath. Feel the warmth and weight of his squirming body. Feel the love he still felt for Rip.

Was this Rip, come back to him? But it wasn't possible, Rip was still alive when these puppies were born.

How did any of this work? Was it magic, was it a miracle, or was it just a coincidence that he wanted to turn into something more?

He looked across the lawn to where Billy Jane held

her puppy across one shoulder like a mother with her baby. She stroked the puppy's back. It looked like the dog was fast asleep.

Tom got up and carried his puppy over to Mrs. Doughty. He kept his voice quiet as he asked her the price.

"Ten dollar each," Mrs. Doughty said.

Tom handed her Ray Swadley's bills.

He carried his puppy over to the girls and asked Billy Jane if she was ready to go back home.

She got a sad look on her face. She started to hand her sleeping puppy to Beth.

"No, her too," Tom said. "I bought them both."

Beth yelped with delight. Billy Jane looked at him in amazement. A smile broke across her pretty face. "Oh, Tom." There were tears shining in her eyes again, but this time they went with the smile.

They both thanked Mrs. Doughty and carried their puppies off toward the road.

Neither of them spoke for what felt like a long time.

"Tom, thank you," Billy Jane said at last. "I'll love her so much."

She hugged the little black body to her chest.

Tom carried his dog more like a sack of potatoes, cradled in both arms and resting against his stomach.

"What should we call them?" Billy Jane asked.

Tom already knew. He knew back when he first picked up the pup.

"Mine's Smoky," he said. It felt right. He couldn't imagine what else he could possibly call him.

"Mine's Stella," Billy Jane said. She bumped her arm against Tom's. He didn't move away, he moved closer to her.

That felt right too.

Back at his house they set the two puppies to play in the grass. Billy Jane and Tom's mother supervised them for a while so Tom could go take care of the rest.

He dismantled his earthen oven. Put the cooked bones back in Sargent's grave and smoothed dirt back on top. He stirred the ashes left over from the fire and buried them with more dirt back into the hole.

He paused for a minute near Rip's grave.

Then he sat down for a quiet chat.

He went through all the memories he wanted to hold, from the time Rip the puppy first looked him in the eye.

All the adventures the two of them had. The good fishing. The many hunts with Tom and his dad.

The way Rip stuck near Tom any time they were out together. How he could have chosen Tom's dad instead, but he picked Tom to be his true master.

His true friend.

Tom felt the same way about Rip.

"Thank you," he whispered to his dog. "You were the best, Rip. I mean it."

He patted the top of Rip's grave and imagined he might be patting the top of Rip's head.

Laughter reached his ears. Billy Jane was lying on the grass while the two puppies crawled all over her.

If Smoky could be even half the dog that Rip was.

Or maybe like Rip, and even better.

No dog was a substitute for another. They were all exactly the dogs they were.

Tom gave Rip's head one final pat, then went off to be with the next one.

A SKIP OF THE MIND

INTRODUCTION

Time travel is real.

The trick is to figure out how to do it without a machine—that will take too long, and the physicist in charge of coming up with the solution is running out of time.

His wife will die if he can't unlock the secret to traveling backward and undoing what has happened.

So why is he fishing instead of working on the problem?

Because sometimes a few days in the wilderness might be just what you need to understand the mysteries of quantum physics.

A tale of the power of science—and the power of love.

A SKIP OF THE MIND

There's a rhythm to camping. You get up, you wonder where you are and why you can't remember, you put on your glasses and they fog up because they've gotten colder in the tent than your face has. And then you see the dog curled up like a worm at the bottom of your sleeping bag, and that already starts the day off right.

But then you do remember. It all comes back. Not just where you are, but why. And that's the tightening of the gut, the unsettling feeling that you meant to invent a time machine over the past few days instead of just fishing in streams.

"Come on, Duke. We have to get back to work."

The two of you stumble out of the tent into the wet grass and both take a long, serious piss. Then the dog stretches like a yogi, yawns wide enough to show his back teeth, and starts looking around for a good stick to chew.

And you fumble around for your pen and the paper that got damp overnight, and it's back to math and equations.

She said you could do it. She said she had faith in you. She reminded you of the time the three of you went back-packing, you and her and the dog, and once you were away and disconnected from all that noise and technology, the ideas burned through and you created the first artificial worm hole. So what, just a tiny one—Jack Smithers came up with that big one last year—but it was something, she said, something new for you, and maybe if you left again you could find the brain capacity that you needed. Because you certainly weren't finding it at home, watching her die.

They say there's a three-day mark—this moment 72 hours into a wilderness experience—when the cares and stresses of society drop off of you like a sheet, and you stand there naked and awake once more.

It's already been four days.

"Let's go catch some breakfast," you tell the dog.

He trots after you through the grass, through the ferns and the willows, down to the river's edge where the fish are hopefully just as stupid and desperate as they were last night.

She might be dead by now.

Don't think about it.

You go through the motions: play out the line, whip the pole back and forth, perfect rhythm, something you could graph and show success rates and line tosses and which fly gets them clambering over each other to snatch it and end up in your frying pan.

There's one. Only took a few casts. Stupid, eager, undiscriminating rainbow trout.

"What d'you think?" you ask Duke, and he does his usual routine of gently nipping at the tip of the fish's tail as you hold it in front of his nose, like he doesn't want to upset you by taking the whole thing, but yeah, he would like just a little taste.

"That one's yours," you tell the dog, and you cast out for another.

If I went back, you think, two weeks—

But is two weeks enough? Maybe the antibodies were there before then—maybe long before. How much? When she was a child? When she was first exposed? When was that?

Fish number two, not as big as the first, but you already promised that first one to the dog. Your fingers burn in the cold water as you gut both fish. Leave the heads and tails on, for no particular reason, since you'll end up throwing those away anyway. It just looks more interesting when their bodies curl up in the frying pan, like they're arching on the end of your line. It's not as dramatic if they're just two stubby lengths of torso. Although when they arch it looks like they're in pain—

"Jake, *go*—"

When she finally sent you away, maybe you were glad to go. Go distract yourself with wilderness and math and physics and build something in your head, instead of just sitting there every day in your cozy house together watching your wife disappear.

"Take the dog and get out," she said, but feebly, so you weren't sure if she really meant it. So you lingered another day, another day when you couldn't do anything to help her. That's when she opened her eyes for a moment, looked clearly into yours, and told you "*Go!*" and this time you believed her.

Because she's a scientist, too. She knows what the mind is capable of when it's relaxed and able to work. And she's scared of dying, it was hard to hide it, and she doesn't want you hanging around when you could be out there doing something about it.

If the infection began when she was first exposed, then what happened right before? Was there a specific event? Can you just erase it?

The whole thing about time travel is it's so easy to mess up. You end up in the wrong version of things, the one over in universe 2.5 instead of 2.4, and in that one you never met and she doesn't know you. She can't comprehend that you just saved her life and now you can go back to being in love. She's with that other guy now, Mr. 2.5, and they're the ones who have children and a life together and so it's no different than if she died. You saved her, but she's still gone.

You spoon the cooked fish, crispy skin and all, into the dog's bowl and eat the smaller one yourself. You pour boiling water into a cup and add microlized coffee and hot chocolate. You snug your cap further down your skull because the wind's picked up, and you try not to think right at it, directly *at* the problem, because that always scares away ideas. You have to think out of the corner of your brain, your peripheral mind, and see what no one else is seeing.

There was that time when you cut yourself badly, and in the stress of the moment you skipped back half a minute before when it didn't happen, and this time you caught yourself before the knife slipped. No monumental shift in the time plates, just a little skip and jump before anyone noticed.

It didn't take a machine. That's where everyone has it wrong. It didn't take metal or math. It was just a wish. A hope. An *oh, shit* and then a ... what? Was it a deliberate thought like, "Go back, go back," or was it a reflex, like putting your arm up to shield yourself against a blow?

Maybe that's it, you think. Maybe you've been thinking too hard. Concentrating on it when it has to be spontaneous. Wishing for it when wishing is the last thing you should do.

It's just a skip of the mind. That's all.

And so you test it. Try it. Don't even worry about the exact time, but just do it, make it a reflex, stop worrying.

You're back on the river bank. Duke is sitting beside you watching while you cast.

Same fish. Same first fish. You can tell by the way it bends the rod, the exact arch of its body against the line.

And this time you throw it back. Don't even let the dog lick its tail. Save the fish that is already technically in the dog's belly, but that was twenty minutes after, and you're not there yet, or you've already been there and come back.

You don't even bother catching the second fish, so its life is spared now too. And then you walk back to camp, and your dog looks at you wondering where breakfast is, but you know he already ate it. Just like those fish are already dead. The dog and the fish don't remember, but you do. Because you made them both happen—the killing and the eating and the not killing.

"Emma."

You're back in your bedroom, with your wife laid out like a corpse, still breathing, but barely. You hopped and skipped back. Dead here soon enough, but alive for another second.

She shouldn't have to suffer anymore in this version of her life. You can help her with that.

You press the pillow over her face. She's so weak she barely even struggles. You don't watch her, try not to even notice. This is something only you will remember, and you don't want to remember too much. That won't do anyone any good.

Then out of the corner of your mind you skip back two weeks, and take her into your arms. You hug her a little longer than the moment calls for, and she laughs a little uncertainly.

"Are you ready?" she asks.

"No, I'm not going. I'm taking you away instead."

"Jake..." She can't believe it. You've been looking forward to this trip with your buddies for so long. But while you're away that weekend she accidentally jabs herself in the lab, gets infected, dies two weeks later by being smothered by a pillow.

Not this time.

"We're going to the mountains," you say. "We'll leave as soon as we can get ready. Come on—let's go."

And when she starts to argue you say, "Trust me." And the way you look at her, the way your eyes narrow at the bottom like you're in pain, the way you squeeze her arm because she *has* to believe you, she has to come—

"Will you tell me?" she asks.

"No."

"Never?"

"Probably never," you say.

But because she knows you, and trusts you, and knows what you're capable of, she nods.

"Okay, I'll go get the gear."

If you can leave by noon, make sure she never goes into the lab, you've made it.

"Hurry," you say.

She looks at you and knows. "I will."

MORE FROM ROBIN BRANDE

SHOW YOUR BOOK-LOVING STYLE!

AND SCIENCE LOVING, ART LOVING, DOG AND CAT LOVING, AND MORE…

Treat yourself to a soft, comfy, custom-made T-shirt designed by Robin Brande herself, inspired by her own books. You can see all of them at robinbrande.com/collections/t-shirts.

And here's a secret just for you: Use the discount code **READER10** at checkout to get **10% off any items in the store.** That means books, T-shirts, hoodies, mugs—whatever you'd like. Go ahead and treat yourself, book lover.

CERTIFIED
BOOK NERD
CERTIFIED
DOG NERD
CERTIFIED
SCIENCE NERD
EMBRACE YOUR NERD
WORTH IT, NERD
NERDS FTW

outside
every
day

science
every
day

brave
every
day

A new full-length Winnie Parsons Mystery Novel

Retired psychology professor Dr. Winifred Parsons spent decades studying the human psyche as a scientist and academic. But she also explored it from another angle: Winnie Parsons is clairvoyant.

Now Winnie's trial lawyer niece, Rose, needs her help with a difficult case. A con man cheated Rose's clients, but how can Rose convince the jury of that?

And why is the judge on the case suddenly lashing out at the lawyers? There are more mysteries than Rose can solve on her own.

The path to justice might be twisted, but Winnie Parsons always finds a way.

Five Winnie Parsons mysteries in one great collection.

- THE GENIUS TRACK: A high school academic star needs Winnie to unlock her troubled mind.
- A MAN OF APPETITES: An ambitious entrepreneur assumes no one can uncover his secrets.
- A DROP OF SWEAT: A cutting-edge scientist hires Winnie to find out who destroyed his lab.
- THE LONG GRAY HOOK: Winnie investigates the medical mystery hobbling the university's dance students.
- THE SLIP OF A RIB: Winnie's work at the local animal shelter leads to a mystery that only she can solve.

X-Files meets *X-Men* in this exciting fantasy and science fiction adventure series by award-winning author Robin Brande.

A POWER SHE DOESN'T WANT. BUT EVERYONE ELSE DOES.

Marnie Stemple has a secret. One she's been able to hide from the world for years. But now she's been exposed. And her worst fears are coming true.

What does the government want from her? To use her as a spy? A weapon? A warrior? She's not made for any of those.

But Marnie can't resist the forces who are after her, any more than she can resist using her power.

Life after death, miracle healings, communication with other species...

- *The Water Healers*: A nurse investigates rumors of miracle healers in Mexico.
- *A Drop of Sweat*: A clairvoyant secretly uses her skills to unravel the mystery of who destroyed a scientist's lab.
- *The Refugees*: A volunteer helps the refugees fleeing a planetary disaster.
- *The Bridge*: A grieving widow refuses to believe her husband is gone forever.
- *The Outpost Away from the World*: A scientist returns to the off-the-grid cabin of her childhood and discovers the mysterious secret to her survival.

ABOUT THE AUTHOR

Robin Brande is an award-winning author, former trial attorney, black belt in martial arts, wilderness medic, and Reiki Master. Her outdoor adventures range from the Rocky Mountains to the Alps to Iceland.

She writes in multiple genres, including young adult, adventure, fantasy, science fiction, mystery, romance, and self-help.

For more information:
robinbrande.com

For information about upcoming new releases, along with previews and special discounts, subscribe to the Robin Brande newsletter. https://robinbrande.com/pages/subscribe.